THE FAERIE GAMES

DARK WORLD: THE FAERIE GAMES 1

MICHELLE MADOW

DREAMSCAPE PUBLISHING

SELENA

I'D ALWAYS HOPED my sixteenth birthday would be the moment I came into my witch powers. That was the way it worked in books and movies, right? You turned a certain age, something important happened, and then BAM.

The magic ignited.

Since I lived on an island full of supernaturals, I should have known better. That wasn't how *our* magic worked. Yet, as the only supernatural on the island that still showed no sign of any magic, I held onto the hope that maybe on this birthday, something would change. I mean, my biological mother was one of the most powerful witches born in the past century.

So why was my magic nonexistent?

No one knew.

I sat in my room in the castle after the party, surrounded by my presents. But I was only focused on the invitation in my hand. It was from the mage Iris— the event coordinator on Avalon—asking me to apprentice by her side for the next two years.

It pissed me off.

A knock on the door pulled me out of my thoughts. I could tell it was my best friend, Torrence, just from the pattern of the raps.

"Come in," I said, dropping the invitation onto my lap.

Torrence waltzed into my room, her long auburn hair flying behind her, and situated herself on the end of my king-size bed. "I knew you were pissed about that one," she said, glancing at the invitation.

"Can you blame me?" I huffed. "Iris is just trying to give me something to do instead of the magic classes I'm barely passing every year."

I would have failed my magic classes if it weren't for the written portions of the tests. Because I understood magic *theory* perfectly well.

Magic *practice*, on the other hand, was a different story.

It was impossible to practice magic when my magic didn't exist.

"Yeah," Torrence agreed. "It sucks."

One of the things I loved about my best friend was that she never sugar coated anything.

I picked up the invitation again and glared at it. As I did, a buzz started from my toes, growing up through my body until it reached my hands. My insides felt like branches of a tree igniting, crackling and popping with electricity.

I gathered the electricity until it was buzzing below the surface of my skin and sent it flying out at the piece of paper in my hand.

In my mind, the paper burst into flames and turned to ashes.

In reality, nothing happened.

"You're staring at that invitation like you expect it to spontaneously combust," Torrence said.

"That's what I just *tried* to do," I said. "I felt the magic. It wants to come out. It's just... stuck."

I shrugged, because this was nothing Torrence hadn't heard before. I'd told everyone about how I could feel the magic inside, wanting to come out. But when the other witches asked me what my magic felt like, they told me it sounded nothing like what their magic felt like when they performed spells.

I didn't think they believed me.

So I'd stopped talking about it. To everyone except

Torrence, of course. Sometimes it felt like she was the only person in the world who still had faith in me.

"There's no spell I've heard of that makes anything spontaneously combust," she said simply. "But if you feel like your magic wants to do that, then hey, it'll be cool to see what you'll be able to do when your magic makes an appearance."

I was grateful that Torrence held out hope that my magic might emerge someday. But I nodded in agreement, since I also knew there wasn't a spell to make things spontaneously combust.

Then I threw the invitation into the fireplace.

Once satisfied that it was burned to a crisp, I leaned back into the mound of pillows behind me, still staring into the flames.

"So..." Torrence said, and I turned my attention back to her. Her green eyes glinted with the look that I knew only meant one thing. Trouble. "The collectors' edition of *Pride and Prejudice* I gave you wasn't your real birthday present."

"It was a great present," I said, since it was. "But now you have me curious. What's my 'real' present?"

Torrence smirked and lifted her hands, chanting a spell I knew well. A sound barrier spell. Her purple magic swirled out of her hands, shooting up to the ceiling and soaring down along the walls as the spell locked into place. The purple disappeared, and now anything we talked about while she maintained the spell wouldn't be overheard.

Each room in the castle already had a sound barrier spell around it, but we liked to be careful. Just in case.

I leaned forward in anticipation. "So?" I asked. "What is it?"

She reached into the sleeve of her sweatshirt and pulled out a vial full of bright red potion.

My eyes widened at the sight of it. "Transformation potion?" I looked to her, to the potion, and back to her again. I didn't need her to nod to confirm what I already knew was true. "What's it for? And where did you get it?"

Transformation potion was one of the hardest potions to create. Only the most advanced witches could brew it. And once it was brewed, it expired after twenty-four hours. So it wasn't something that was kept in storage.

"I made it, using my own blood," she said. "So you can transform into me."

2

SELENA

"Why would I want to transform into you?" I asked, confused.

Nothing against my bestie. She was awesome. But as much as I admired and appreciated Torrence, I didn't want to *be* her. I was perfectly happy being myself.

Except for my missing magic. But that couldn't be fixed with transformation potion. Transformation potion would make me look like Torrence on the outside, but I'd still be me on the inside. Missing magic and all.

"Other than your magic igniting, what's the one thing you want most in the entire world?" Torrence asked.

"To be allowed off of Avalon." I didn't have to stop to

think about my answer. "But my parents won't allow it. You know the rules. They won't let me—"

I cut myself off, the pieces clicking together as I stared at the bright red potion in Torrence's hand.

"They won't let *you* off the island," she completed my thought. "But I can come and go as I please. Like I do every weekend when I visit my mom in LA."

"You really think it would work?" My eyes widened, my heart racing with excitement and anticipation. "That I could pretend to be you and leave the island? Just like that?"

My entire life, my parents had drilled it into my mind that I'd never be able to leave Avalon. My mom was an Earth Angel—the only one in the world, and she was the leader of our island.

So many people on Earth—demons and supernaturals alike—would come after me if I stepped foot off this island. They'd want to take me and use me as leverage against my mom. Combined with the fact that my magic was non-existent, giving me no way to defend myself, it was too risky for me to leave.

Which meant I had to stay here. Forever.

That was a long time. Especially since because of the island's magic, once we reached our mid-twenties, we stopped aging and became immortal.

I held out hope that at some point in the future, Earth would be peaceful enough that I'd be allowed to see it myself. But until that time came, this island was all I'd see and experience.

I loved Avalon. I had a great life here. But even though I loved it, I still wanted to see the world.

And right now, Torrence was giving me that chance.

"I know it'll work." Torrence's eyes sparkled with mischief again. "You know me better than anyone. If anyone can convince my mom that they're me, it's you."

"Maybe," I said, since it wasn't a terrible idea. "But we'll need to practice."

"There's no time for that," she said. "It has to be this weekend."

"Why?" I asked. "I mean, I know the potion expires after twenty-four hours. But you created it once. Couldn't you create it again?"

"Of course I can create it again." She tossed her hair over her shoulders, like it was silly of me to even ask. "But along with expiring after twenty-four hours in the vial, the potion will only keep you transformed for twenty-four hours after drinking it. And you know the deal I made with my mom when I was accepted onto Avalon."

"You can attend the academy here as long as you visit her every weekend." I was the one who'd suggested

Torrence offer her mom that deal when her mom was hesitating about letting her go to school here. Torrence and I had clicked the moment we'd met, and I hated the idea of her not being able to stay. Having her here five days out of seven was better than nothing at all.

"Even though it's Friday, I was able to stay tonight because there was no way I was missing your birthday," she said. "Which means my visit home will be cut short this weekend. I head back tomorrow. Well... *you'll* head back tomorrow. As me." She pressed the pads of her fingers together, like a conniving villain in a superhero movie.

My head spun with excitement... and with all the possible ways this could go wrong.

"What's up?" Torrence asked, dropping her hands back down to her sides.

She knew me well enough to know I'd have questions. And knowing her, she'd already thought about what I'd ask and what the answers to those questions would be.

"A bunch of stuff," I said. "Firstly, thank you. This gift is amazing."

"I know." She smiled proudly.

"But how will I get to LA? I have no magic. I can't teleport."

"I'll teleport you straight to my room," she said. "I

always drop my stuff off there first, anyway. Then I'll pop back to LA the next day and take you home."

"Okay." I nodded, since that worked. "But I can't do magic, and the transformation potion won't change that. Won't your mom wonder what's up if I need to do magic and I can't?"

"My mom's *always* telling me I should rest my magic more so I'm fresh and ready for the school week." Torrence rolled her eyes. She loved using her magic, but preferred using it for personal use instead of for classroom exercises. "Just tell her there's a big test on Monday and that you're resting your magic so you're ready. She'll be thrilled. That'll be your reason for coming home earlier on Sunday, too. You need to study for the test."

The test that didn't exist.

"All right." I nodded again, liking the sound of this more and more. "But what about me? And by that I mean the lack of me here on Avalon. People will notice if I'm gone. Especially since my parents' big anniversary dinner is tomorrow night."

"Easy." Torrence shrugged. "I'll create another transformation potion tonight, using your blood. It'll be ready by tomorrow. I'll drink it and take your place while you're gone."

"So we're swapping places." I sat forward, unable to help laughing at how crazy this all was. It was also perfect. Because if any two people knew each other well enough to swap places and pull it off, it was me and Torrence.

"Exactly." She smiled again. "You in?"

"I am," I said, since how could I not be? The possibility of twenty-four hours off of Avalon was the most exciting thing to happen to me since... well, it was the most exciting thing to *ever* happen to me. "But what happens if we're caught?"

I already knew the answer to that.

Anyone caught trying to get me off Avalon would be accused of treason. There were no set punishments for anything here—punishments were decided on an individual basis. But treason wouldn't be taken lightly.

"Are you doubting that the potion will work?" She raised an eyebrow in question.

"No," I said. "You're one of the best witches on this island. I'm sure it'll work."

"So what's the problem?"

"I'm just trying to think everything through," I said. "So we don't make any mistakes."

"No one will notice that we're not who we say we are," she said. "I can be you. You can be me. No one knows that I know how to make transformation potion, so they won't think this is even a possibility. Everyone on Avalon will be too focused on your parents' anniversary celebration to be paying attention to me. My mom's used to my mood swings, so she won't notice anything different with you. And it's only twenty-four hours. What could possibly happen in twenty-four hours that would get us caught?"

"I don't know," I said, my stomach doing somersaults at the realization that this was going to happen. I was going to see the world beyond Avalon. Sure, it would only be a sliver of the big world out there, but it was still more than I ever thought possible.

"We'd have to mess up *badly* to get caught," she said. "And we're not going to do that. You're going to see LA, and you're going to have a great time. No one will ever know you were gone."

"I guess." I did my best to squash down the worry in my stomach.

This was a once-in-a-lifetime opportunity. Was I really going to say no because I was scared?

Hell no, I wasn't.

So I buried the worry so deep that all I could focus on was my excitement. "You definitely win the prize for best-present ever," I said, nearly squealing with anticipation.

"Told you so." She beamed. "Now, give me your hand so I can take your blood. Transformation potion isn't the easiest thing to make, and I need to have the second vial ready by tomorrow."

3

SELENA

THE NEXT DAY, Torrence teleported back into my room right after lunch. She had bags under her eyes and her hair was in a messy bun at the top of her head, like she hadn't slept all night. But she dropped her bag on the trunk at the end of the bed, reached in, and pulled out two vials of bright red potion. One was marked with a T, and the other was marked with an S.

"Two vials of transformation potion," she said, handing me the one with the S on it. "As promised."

Despite looking tired, she sounded as excited as ever. She pulled off her clothes, revealing her skintight, black academy uniform underneath. The academy uniforms were spelled with special magic that would mold with shapeshifting. I was already in mine.

I uncapped my vial and held it up for a toast.

Torrence did the same.

"To the best birthday present ever," I said.

"To twenty-four hours of adventure." Torrence smiled and clinked her vial with mine.

We brought the vials to our lips and drank them at the same time.

The transformation potion tasted sweet, like raspberry, and it fizzed on my tongue. The fizzing quickly expanded down into my throat, into my stomach, and out toward my fingers and toes.

Torrence blurred in front of me, the lines around her body becoming hazy. Her auburn hair turned blond, she became shorter, and her sharp green eyes turned violet.

She'd transformed into me.

"Whoa," Torrence said, looking at me. "That's sick."

I moved to stand in front of my full-length mirror. Sure enough, it wasn't myself staring back at me.

It was Torrence.

I reached up to touch my cheek, watching as Torrence's reflection in the mirror mimicked my movement.

"It worked," I said, surprised when the voice coming out of my mouth wasn't my own. It was Torrence's, although her voice sounded slightly different from inside her head. A bit lower pitched.

"I wouldn't give you a birthday present that didn't

work," she said. "Now, are you going to change into my clothes or what? Because you only have twenty-four hours as me, and the clock started ticking the moment you finished that potion."

Once I'd changed into Torrence's clothes, she teleported me into her bedroom in LA. She had a pink comforter, a shelf full of kids' books, and matching pink, frilly drapes.

It was a bedroom for a ten-year-old.

"I guess you haven't redecorated since coming to Avalon?" I asked with a laugh.

"Nah." She shrugged. "I'm not here that often, so oh well."

This was so weird. My best friend looked like me... but she still had that wicked glint in her eyes. *My* eyes. Although I was sure I'd never looked as mischievous as that.

"Don't do anything *too* crazy while you're pretending to be me," I said. "No flirting with guys or anything like that. Got it?"

The last thing I wanted was to get back home and have to deal with any drama Torrence left in my wake.

"I promise I won't do anything crazy, like flirting

with guys." The sarcasm in her tone made it clear she didn't think flirting was crazy, although I knew she'd keep her word and respect my wishes. "But I'll totally plant some seeds in Reed's mind that'll make him interested in me."

"Of course you will," I said, since there was no way of stopping her. Torrence was doing a lot for me this weekend. If she wanted to have her fun and plant seeds in Reed's mind, then that was what she'd do.

"He's not married yet," she said. "He's still fair game."

Suddenly, she jerked her head to the side, instantly alert.

Now that we were both quiet, I heard what she'd already picked up on.

Someone was walking down the hall.

"That's my mom," she said quickly. "I gotta blink out. Cya tomorrow!"

I didn't have a chance to say bye before she teleported out of her room.

A few seconds later, Amber—Torrence's mom— knocked on the door. At least I assumed it was Amber, since that was what Torrence had said.

I needed to remember to call her Mom while I was here. It would be strange, but I could do it.

"Come in," I said, trying to imitate Torrence's blasé yet confident tone.

The door swung open, and sure enough, Torrence's mom stood in the entrance. She wore light jeans and a pink tank, and her blond hair was up in a high ponytail.

Amber looked more like me than the pictures I'd seen of my biological mother.

Except for my violet eyes. No one was sure where *those* came from. A genetic mutation was the best guess.

"I thought I heard you pop in," she said with a warm smile. "I had breakfast ready a bit ago, but you're later than expected. It's probably cold now."

"We stayed up super late after Selena's birthday party and I slept through my alarm." I shrugged, giving the story Torrence and I had planned ahead of time. "Sorry."

"No worries," she said. "Want to head downstairs? I can whip up something else, if you're hungry."

"Actually, I was hoping we could go out to brunch," I said. "And then maybe to the beach? We could do a mother-daughter day and explore like we used to."

"I like that plan." Amber smiled. "When do you want to leave?"

"Now." I bounced on my toes in anticipation of my first day experiencing the world beyond Avalon.

This really was the best birthday present ever.

4

SELENA

My mother-daughter day with Amber was *amazing*. She had no idea I wasn't Torrence, which meant I was playing my part perfectly.

When we got back, we had dinner with Torrence's aunts—Evangeline and Doreen—on the outside patio. But it eventually grew late, and the others went up to their rooms to go to bed.

I went back to Torrence's room, but I was too amped up to get ready for bed. I only had twenty-four hours, and I didn't want to waste a single minute of it sleeping.

Unfortunately, there were gates and magical shields around the property. And while I wanted adventure, it would be stupid to explore LA at night alone. This city could be dangerous. Especially at night.

It looked like I was stuck staying in.

But just because I was stuck on the property, it didn't mean I had to stay in Torrence's room.

So I padded down the hallway toward the stairs. The three witches' lights were off and there were no sounds from their rooms. They were fast asleep.

Once outside, I walked past the gorgeous fountain in the driveway and up to the gate at the end of it, placing my hands on the metal bars. The gate was supposed to be sealed shut. But it moved after the slightest pressure of my hand and slid silently open, as if beckoning me forward.

I stared at the gate in surprise. That wasn't supposed to happen.

Curious, I headed out of the gate and down the driveway. I wasn't going to actually try walking anywhere, but it could be fun to watch the cars drive by. We didn't have cars on Avalon, so just looking at the different varieties of cars they had in LA was interesting.

But when I walked to the end of the long driveway, I saw someone standing at the end of the driveway next door. His back was toward me. He was tall with dark blond hair, and he was wearing jeans and a black leather jacket.

He turned around, and the moment his bright blue

eyes met mine, warmth burst from my chest and traveled through every inch of my body.

He looked to be around my age, maybe a bit older. And from the intense way he was staring at me, I wondered if I was somehow having the same effect on him that he was having on me.

But he snapped out of it, shooting me a devilish smile that made my heart race faster. "Torrence Devereux," he said my best friend's name, his voice like music to my ears.

Like a siren's call beckoning me closer.

How could Torrence have never mentioned her ridiculously hot neighbor? That wasn't like her at all.

Maybe he wasn't hot until recently? That happened a lot with guys. They had an awkward phase, they grew out of it, and then BOOM. Sudden hotness.

But I was staring. I needed to say something— anything—so he didn't think I was a mute freak.

"Have we met before?" I asked once I had my wits somewhat together.

"We used to play together as kids," he said. "You don't remember?"

"It was a long time ago." It seemed as good of an answer as any.

"It was." He nodded, his enchanting gaze locked on mine. "You're not around here often anymore, are you?"

"I go to a year-round boarding school up north." It was Torrence's cover-story, so I didn't have to think twice about that one. "I'm only here on the weekends."

"Got it," he said. "So… what are your plans for the rest of the night?"

I glanced back at Torrence's house. The windows on the second floor were still dark. "Nothing." I shrugged. "My mom and aunts went to sleep, but I wasn't tired."

"So you wandered to the end of your driveway." He chuckled, that knowing twinkle still in his eyes.

"Yeah." My cheeks heated, since it sounded ridiculous when he put it that way. I needed to switch the conversation away from me and my weirdness, quickly. "What about you?" I asked. "Why are you just standing here?"

"I'm heading out to hang with some friends. My Uber should be here in…" He paused to glance at his phone. "Three minutes."

"Oh." I deflated at the realization that he was leaving soon.

Of course he was leaving.

Normal people didn't wander down to the end of their driveway to watch the cars go by.

And I was doing a terrible job at pretending to be Torrence right now. Torrence always knew what to say around guys she was interested in. But none of the guys on Avalon had ever interested me as anything more than a friend, so I'd never thought about it much.

Now I finally met someone who took my breath away, and he was a human who lived on Earth. A place I could never return to. And I was meeting him as Torrence—not as me.

Just my awful luck.

"Do you want to come?" he asked.

"Out?" I blinked, sure I'd misunderstood. "With you and your friends?"

"I can ditch my friends tonight," he said. "I mean, I haven't seen you in years. We should catch up. Just the two of us."

Sometime while we'd been talking, we'd inched onto the yard between our driveways until we were standing a few feet away from each other. His eyes were an even brighter blue up close. Ice blue, although they somehow managed to be warm at the same time.

"Just the two of us," I repeated, a small smile creeping over my lips. I might as well go for it. I had nothing to lose. "Like, on a date?"

"Yes." He didn't pause for a second. "I'd like to go on a date with you. If that's okay with you, of course."

From the way he was looking at me—like he was seeing all the way into my soul—I had a feeling he knew it was *more* than okay with me.

I wanted to say yes.

But going out with a stranger was reckless.

He's not a stranger, I reminded myself. *He's Torrence's neighbor. They played together when they were kids.*

And he was looking at me like my answer meant the world to him.

I had no idea what to do. But wasn't this the point of swapping places with my best friend? To be reckless? To have experiences I'd never have on Avalon?

Something—perhaps fate—pulled me toward him, urging me to say yes. I didn't think I could walk away at this point even if I wanted to.

"You never told me your name," I realized. "I can't go out on a date with you if I don't know your name."

"My name's Julian," he said, and warm tingles ran up and down my spine at his voice.

"Julian," I repeated, his name sounding like music when I spoke it aloud. "Yes. I'd love to go on a date with you."

5

SELENA

WE HOPPED into the Uber and slid into the back seat.

"Change of plans," Julian told the driver. "We're heading to Trevi Square."

The driver nodded, inputted the new destination in his navigation system, and we were off.

"What's at Trevi Square?" I asked Julian. The center seat between us was empty, and a part of me wished I'd sat there instead, just to be closer to him.

"It's an area nearby with a bunch of restaurants," he answered simply. "It's a cool place to hang out."

Was it just my imagination, or did I see a flicker of guilt in his eyes?

But then he smiled, and I knew I must have imagined it.

"I was thinking we could grab dessert," he continued. "They have some great gelato places."

"That sounds perfect." I smiled, since it did.

"Great," he said. "Then dessert it is."

Trevi Square was just like Julian had described—a bunch of restaurants surrounding a large fountain in the middle. The fountain was built to look like the Trevi Fountain in Rome—it was huge, with beautiful statues of gods and creatures from mythology around it. I recognized it from pictures and movies, although of course I'd never been to the real one myself.

We grabbed gelato and sat at the benches near the fountain, watching people walk by and throw coins in the water.

"So," Julian said after a fair bit of chatting while we ate. "Why do you go to boarding school up north when there are tons of great schools here in LA?"

Torrence had a cover-up story I knew by heart.

But I didn't want to keep pretending around Julian. He hadn't seen Torrence since they were kids, so he had no expectation of what she was like.

I wanted him to see *me*. Not Torrence. There was nothing I could do about the fact that I looked like her, but I wanted something about this night to feel genuine. I wanted Julian to see my soul—the person I was beneath the mask of my best friend.

Well, I wanted him to see as much of myself as I could share without mentioning the supernatural world.

"This boarding school is special," I started, creating the story in my mind as I went along. "It's intensely focused on sports. You see, everyone in my family is super athletic. They expect the same from me."

If by "athletic" I meant that they were all gifted with magic they could actually use, then yeah.

"But you're not happy there?" He scooted closer, looking at me like my answer meant the world to him.

"It's not that," I said. "I'm happy. Everyone there is great. And I want to excel in sports, like the way they want me to. But I'm just…" I paused, searching for the right word to get across the general idea without telling the exact truth. "I'm not gifted like they are. And to be honest, I'm starting to feel like I never will be."

"So sports aren't your calling," he said. "That's okay. There's no point in sitting around wanting to be something you're not. All you can do is focus on what you *are* good at and go from there."

His response was surprisingly understanding. "You sound like you know a bit about this yourself," I said, placing my finished cup of gelato down next to me.

"My family expects a lot from me, too." His eyes went distant as he stared out at the fountain. "But it's more than that. They *need* a lot from me. You see, my sister— my twin—is sick. A chronic stomach thing. There's no cure."

"I'm so sorry." My heart went out to him. Especially because while there wasn't a human cure, there might be a magical one.

Once I got back to Avalon, I'd talk to Torrence about it. Maybe she could get her mom and aunts to create a potion for Julian's sister that would help her. Without Julian and his sister knowing it was magic, of course. They'd say it was herbs, or something.

"I hate seeing her like that," he said. "She'll never be able to live the way she wants to. She'll most likely never be able to support herself. So the pressure's on me to live for both of us. To do everything I can to make sure she never has to worry about anything. Even if those decisions take away from my own happiness. Even if they're the hardest decisions I'll ever have to make in my life." He watched me intensely, like he *needed* me to understand.

"That sounds hard," I said, and he just nodded, turning to stare blankly out at the fountain.

Talking about his sister was clearly upsetting him.

Time to change the subject.

"So, what's your ring stand for?" I asked, motioning to the chunky band around his right ring finger. It was inscribed with words—Latin, it looked like, although I wouldn't be able to make them out unless it was right in front of my face. "It looks important."

"That's because it *is* important." He focused on me again, although he lowered the hand with the ring on it down to his side. "It was a gift from someone with a lot of influence. A promise that I'll be given an opportunity for greatness. An opportunity to make sure my sister never has to worry about anything again."

I wasn't exactly sure what he meant. But then he placed his nearly finished ice cream down and focused on me, like I was the only person in the world who mattered to him. His gaze was intense, and my breathing shallowed, my eyes locked on his stunning light blue ones.

"I'm really happy to have had this night with you," he said, each word full of meaning that I had the feeling I was barely touching the surface of understanding. It was almost like he knew—as I did—that we'd never see each other again.

I was about to say I was happy we'd had this night together, too, but before I had the chance, he moved closer and gently lowered his lips to mine.

6

SELENA

ELECTRICITY HUMMED THROUGH MY BODY, as if Julian's touch had awakened the magic I knew was in there. Every inch of my skin prickled with awareness, and I leaned in, pressing my lips harder to his in encouragement.

He pulled me closer and deepened the kiss. He tasted sweet, like vanilla and honey, and I savored every moment that we were together. It was like our bodies *knew* each other, even though that was impossible.

Julian was lighting my soul on fire, and I never wanted this moment to end.

But all good things had to end. So eventually, he pulled away.

I gazed up at him, and my lips parted, craving more of him.

How could I feel so connected to someone I'd only met a few hours ago? It made no sense. And yet, it was there. Like a bolt of lightning fusing his heart to mine, jolting my soul awake with emotions and feelings too sudden and strong to fully understand.

At the same time, my chest hollowed at the knowledge that I'd never see him again. The emptiness *hurt*. I missed him already, even though he was still next to me.

He looked at me like he was in a trance. Whatever I was feeling, he was feeling it, too. I didn't know how I knew it. I just did.

Then he became more focused, his fingers grazing my cheek as he studied me. His eyes were full of so many conflicting emotions. Like he couldn't settle on just one.

I looked up at him in question, also unable to put my racing emotions into words. How could I, when I couldn't tell him who I truly was, and why I was actually here? When I couldn't tell him that next weekend, the Torrence who came back wouldn't be me, but someone else entirely?

When I returned to Avalon, I'd be leaving a part of myself behind with Julian. And knowing that felt like a fistful of daggers piercing my heart at once.

From the pained look in his eyes, I suspected he felt the same.

But then, his expression changed into something else.

Resolve.

He reached into his pocket and pulled out two golden coins. "We should make a wish," he said slowly. "In the fountain."

I reached for one of the coins and picked it up to take a closer look. It was gold, the front of it engraved into a detailed profile of a man. He had a strong jaw, hair nearly to his shoulders, and a wreath around his head. The word *Devyn* curved around the side, along with a few other letters that meant nothing to me.

"What type of money is this?" I asked, since I knew enough about American coins to know this wasn't one of them.

"They're euros," he said quickly. "From a trip to Italy I took this summer."

"Are you sure you want to waste them on a wish?" I said it jokingly, but the coins looked valuable. Like something he'd want to hold onto.

"It wouldn't be a waste," he said, closing my hand around the coin. "Maybe because they're euros, our wishes will be more likely to come true. What do we have to lose?" He reached for my other hand and took it in his, raising me up to my feet and leading me toward the fountain. Once we were there, he stepped up onto the ledge and helped me up, too. It was like we were gods staring down at the shimmering water below.

I held the coin tighter, since he was right. I might as well toss it into the fountain and make my wish count.

"Are you ready?" he asked, a flash of dark intensity crossing his eyes as he stared down at me.

It was like he was daring me to say no.

"Yes," I said determinedly, my other hand still locked with his. We hadn't broken contact with each other since the kiss.

"Perfect," he said, although he didn't sound like he believed it. "Let's throw them on the count of three."

I wasn't sure why he sounded so torn about this. It was just a wish. It was fun and all, but it wasn't like the wish would actually come true.

Still, I *wanted* it to be able to come true.

So I nodded, and he counted off. After three, we tossed our coins up in the air.

As mine arced upward, I thought, *I wish I'll get to continue seeing Julian after tonight.*

I saw him staring at his coin, and I knew he was making his wish, too.

The coins plopped into the water at the same time. And suddenly, as if they'd released a potion, purple leaked out from the coins and into the water like smoke. The purple grew brighter and more intense, until the entire pool glowed, sparkled, and swirled like a galaxy of glittering stars.

I stared at it in shock.

My magic must have done something. I'd felt my magic stronger than ever when Julian had kissed me.

Had his kiss brought my magic to the surface?

It must have. I couldn't believe it. I'd waited all my life for my magic to emerge. And now, it was finally happening. When I was on Earth, pretending to be my best friend, and sneaking out behind her mom's back to go on a date with her mysterious, magnetic neighbor.

Worst. Timing. Ever.

How was I supposed to explain my magic to this gorgeous human guy who had no idea the supernatural world existed?

I looked up at Julian, unsure what to say.

The purple glow lit up his face. But he didn't look surprised. In fact, he was completely calm. Eerily so.

As if he knew this was going to happen.

"I'm sorry, Selena," he said, and then he jumped into the glowing purple water, his hand that was still holding onto mine pulling me along with him.

7

SELENA

RIGHT BEFORE HITTING THE WATER, I had the sense to close my eyes and hold my breath.

Except I didn't hit any water.

I became weightless. Like I was floating through space.

I opened my eyes and saw the swirling purple galaxy around me. Then it disappeared into mist.

The next thing I knew, I was on solid ground, and the mist cleared. It was early morning, and I was on my knees in front of a fountain in the courtyard of a strange, foreign house. The courtyard was surrounded by columns, all with colorful leaves and flowering vines twisted around them.

Julian was on his knees beside me, his hand still holding onto mine. And standing before us was a man with shoulder-length platinum blond hair, violet eyes that looked like mine, pointed ears, and wings. Bright green wings that looked more like lines of sparkling light than solid matter. They were unearthly and beautiful, unlike anything I'd ever seen.

Whoever this man was, he was clearly supernatural. But there was no record in any of our history books about supernaturals with wings like his.

Refocusing on his face, I realized I recognized it. It was the same face that was engraved on the coin Julian had given me to make a wish in the fountain.

The man now had both coins in his hands, and he placed them in his pocket. He wore loose green pants that I could only describe as breeches, with a matching tunic. Both the pants and tunic had intricately woven patterns in them that were threaded with gold.

Two men stood behind him. Both had no wings, were dressed in plain brown garb, and had matching red bands tattooed around the tops of their right arms.

Where was I? Who were these people? Why was I here?

Despite my confusion, I forced myself to stand. I had no idea what was going on or how I'd gotten there, but I'd face these people with dignity.

Julian stood along with me.

"Julian," the winged man said before I could speak

my questions out loud. "Good job bringing my daughter home."

He knew Julian's name.

Which meant Julian had pulled me into that glowing purple water and brought me here—which judging from this strange man's accent, was somewhere in England—on purpose. He'd lied to me.

Yet, I still held onto his hand. Touching him felt as natural as breathing. Like he was the only solid thing I had left to hold onto.

But my strange infatuation with him was clearly ruining my ability to make good decisions.

So I yanked my hand out of his, trying to ignore the coldness that shuddered through my body as it protested against my letting go. I moved to push my hair out of my face, and that was when I realized—my hair was blond again.

I'd returned to my true form. That strange purple water must have stripped the transformation potion from my body.

I didn't know any spells strong enough to do that.

Wherever I was, I needed to get out of there. Fast.

I met the man's gaze, my upbringing as a princess of Avalon taking hold at once. "I'm not your daughter," I said, since that was something I was sure of. "My parents are Queen Annika and Prince Jacen of Avalon. I need to return home immediately, before they wonder where I am and send the Nephilim to find me." I let threat linger in my voice for the last part. Everyone in the supernatural world feared the Nephilim.

But the man with the green wings didn't even flinch at the mention of them.

"You are Selena Pearce." He held his violet gaze—his eyes so similar to my own—with mine. "Raised by Queen Annika and Prince Jacen of Avalon. But you're the biological daughter of the late Camelia Conrad, former head witch of the Vale, and myself. Devyn Kavanagh, faerie prince of the Otherworld. It's a pleasure to finally meet you."

"You're mistaken." It took all of my effort to keep my irritation from my tone. Because I'd know if I were half fae. My parents wouldn't have lied to me about something so huge. "Not about Camelia Conrad. You're correct that she was my biological mother. But my biological father was a witch slaughtered in the Battle at the Vale."

"Wrong." The man—Prince Devyn—smirked. "I'm your father." I opened my mouth to argue against him, but he continued before I could. "I'm sure you have many questions. But first, I have business to take care of." He reached into his other pocket and pulled out a cloth bag tied at the top with twine. It appeared to be heavy with coins. "Julian. Your payment for bringing her to me, as promised." He tossed the bag toward Julian, who caught it easily with one hand. "Now, stop standing there and be on your way."

Julian looked at me, his eyes pained. "Selena," he said, and I realized this wasn't the first time he'd said my true name.

He'd said it right before pulling me into the fountain.

He'd known I wasn't Torrence the whole time.

"I'm so sorry." He spoke faster, desperate now. His accent was different from the one he'd used back in LA. More British than American. "But remember what I told you about my sister. I had to do this. For her."

"You lied to me." My rage crackled like electricity under my skin. "You *abducted* me."

He'd used me. He'd traded me for money. Like I was a thing and not a person.

I hated him.

He must have seen the hate strewn across my face, because his entire demeanor changed. He was stiffer than before. It was like his mind was further away, and harder to reach.

"You have a home here," he said. "You're one of us. This is where you belong."

His words sent shivers down my spine, and not in a good way. Because the Otherworld wasn't my home.

39

My home was Avalon.

And I was going to get back there. I didn't know exactly how I'd get back, but I'd figure it out. If nothing else, I needed to stay alive long enough for my parents to find me and rescue me.

"Enough." Devyn set his hard eyes on Julian. "Leave at once, or the money is no longer yours."

Julian clenched his jaw, anguish all over his face once more. When he looked at me, the message he was trying to get across was as plain as day.

He was sorry.

I raised my chin in defiance. Because I'd never forgive him. And after what he did to me, I had nothing more to say to him.

Prince Devyn took a threatening step toward Julian.

Then, with one final pained look in my direction, Julian pulled the bag of money to his chest, turned around, and left.

8

JULIAN

I HURRIED to the outskirts of the city. The bag of gold—now with slightly fewer coins in it—was in one of my pockets.

The expensive herbs that helped Vita's sickness were in the other. I'd purchased the herbs in the forum in the center of the city, where the fae lived in their luxurious city houses.

The further I got from the center of the city, the smaller the houses became. Eventually they turned into the insula apartments for half-bloods like me. And as I walked through the narrow streets, my mind went to the one place it now seemed incapable of staying away from.

To Selena.

I'd been prepped for the mission going in. I knew

that Prince Devyn's daughter, Selena, would be in LA disguised as a witch named Torrence Devereux. I knew everything to do, including using the potion bomb full of fae magic to unlock the gate outside the Devereux house so Selena would be able to leave. I knew precisely when Selena would walk down that driveway, and I'd been positioned there to do exactly what I'd done—take her to a nearby fountain, earn her trust, convince her to toss Prince Devyn's token into the water, and then pull her through the portal and into the Otherworld with me.

But I hadn't expected to have my breath taken away at the sight of her. I hadn't expected to have *wanted* to kiss her, and then to have it be the most intoxicating kiss of my life.

After kissing Selena, I wasn't sure I'd be able to kiss anyone else ever again. I wasn't sure I'd want to.

And then, when we came through the portal and the magic stripped away her transformation potion… I was transfixed. Torrence was a beautiful girl, there was no doubt about it.

But Selena was mesmerizing, with her bright blond hair, thoughtful violet eyes, and perfectly pink lips. I'd wanted to pull her toward me and kiss her again, to feel and taste her in her true form. I had no idea how it could be more magical than that first kiss, but with her, I had a feeling it could be possible.

If we hadn't been surrounded by Prince Devyn and his guards, I *would* have kissed her again. I ached just thinking about her.

But I shook the thoughts of Selena from my mind. I had no business thinking that way about Prince Devyn's daughter. Not when I had more pressing matters to concern myself with.

As I continued along the streets, the apartments got more and more rundown as I reached the end of the city limits. If anyone passing by had a clue as to what valuables I had in my pockets, they'd try to steal from me on the spot.

Try being the key word. Because they'd fail. I'd been training in combat since I was a kid. No half-blood in the city stood a chance against me.

Once I reached the decrepit, tall apartment building that I called home, I hurried up to the top floor where I lived with my mom and sister and opened the door into the single room we shared.

My sister was curled up in her bed with a blanket wrapped around her, her face contorted in pain as cold sweat dripped down the sides of her cheeks. My mom held a wet rag to her forehead to try soothing her. But I knew it wouldn't help.

"Vita," I said my sister's name and hurried to the stove to start heating up the water. "I have your medicine. It'll be okay soon."

I emptied the herbs onto a chopping board, and my mom walked to my side to prepare it. She only took a portion for now—the rest would be saved for later.

"There's been talk around town," my mom said as she set about grinding the herbs into tea leaves. "They're worried that Vita has the Wild Plague."

"The Wild Plague doesn't exist." I gave my mom a stern look, wishing she'd stop believing every rumor that spread around the citadel.

The last thing she needed to do was to upset Vita with lies.

"That's not what people are saying," she said. "The baker's son has a friend who says his cousin was out in the Wild Lands recently. He saw one of them. A fae with the Wild Plague. He said the fae had turned into a monster. His wings were black and dead, and his eyes were milky white, like he had no soul."

"And what happened to the cousin of a friend of the baker's son?" I didn't believe the crazy story for a second, but it never hurt to ask questions.

"He ran back home," she said. "Apparently there was some kind of boundary keeping the soulless fae from following him."

Her story sounded more ridiculous by the second. "Even if this happened," I started, making it clear in my tone that I didn't believe it did, "Why would people say Vita has the Wild Plague? She's had her condition since she was a child. Everyone knows that."

"People are scared." My mom's eyes—the same ice blue ones as my own—darkened. "When people get scared, they like to talk. They want to place blame somewhere. Those who are weak or different are easy targets."

Weak or different. Vita was both of those things.

But Vita didn't have to be this way. If the herbs that helped her weren't so expensive, she'd be able to live and work like the rest of us.

Which was why I was doing everything in my power to make sure we'd be able to afford her medicine—and everything else we'd ever need—for the rest of our lives.

As we waited for the tea to ready, I emptied the bag of coins and counted the gold inside of it. "There's enough here to keep getting her medicine for a few weeks," I said. "And to hold you over with food while I'm playing in the Games."

My mom's hand shot out, and she wrapped her fingers tightly around my wrist. "There's enough gold in there to hold all three of us over for months," she said.

"Maybe more, if we're careful. You don't have to enter the Games."

"I'm entering the Games." I'd had this conversation with her enough times. There was no need to rehash it again. "And, gods willing, I'll be chosen to play in them. It's the only way to secure our future. Permanently."

It was the only way to make sure we'd have enough money to afford the herbs Vita needed to live a life free of pain. It was the only way for my sister to *have* a future. At least, one worth living.

"You'll be killed." My mother's eyes went to the portrait of my father—the only piece of art we had in our measly home.

The portrait was drawn right after the god Mars had chosen my father to play in the Faerie Games. My father stood proud with his shiny, steel-colored wings behind him, ready to compete in the Games that would eventually take his life.

My sister and I had only been a year old at the time. According to people who'd known my mom back then, she hadn't been the same since his death.

"I can't lose you." She looked away from the portrait, shaking her head in grief. "Not after losing him."

"I've been training for this my whole life." I kept my gaze leveled on hers, willing her to be strong. She'd have to be, when I was away from home and playing in the Games. "I'll win."

"Your father thought he would win, too."

My father's memory hung heavy in the air between us.

"Father relied only on brawn," I said exactly what I'd been telling her for over a year. "I have both brawn *and* strategy. I'm ready for this. I'm going to win."

I finished preparing Vita's tea in silence, not wanting to harp on the past. My father had died playing in the Faerie Games, trying to provide a better life for his family.

History wasn't going to repeat itself.

Because I was going to succeed where my father had failed.

And I refused to let any distractions—like Selena Pearce—get in the way of my goal.

9

SELENA

"FOLLOW ME TO THE DINING ROOM," Prince Devyn said—no, *commanded*. "There's breakfast waiting for us. We have much to discuss."

I glanced at the fountain I'd portaled in through. Then I sprinted toward it and jumped inside.

Water splashed up at me. My shoes and bottom halves of my jeans were soaked. But I hadn't gone anywhere. I was still in the courtyard of this strange Roman-style house. And now I was wet.

I cursed under my breath. I'd hoped I could jump in the fountain and end up back in LA.

"Portals only work in conjunction with a faerie token," Prince Devyn said, his hand going to the pocket where he'd placed the tokens Julian and I had used to arrive. "Otherwise, they're just normal fountains. Step out, please. I don't imagine it's comfortable in there."

Standing in the fountain, soaking wet and looking like an idiot wasn't doing me any good. So I stepped out of the fountain, making sure not to let defeat show on my face.

"I want to return home." I eyed the pocket where he was keeping the faerie tokens. "What deal do you want to make in exchange for one of those tokens?"

I knew about faeries and their deals. They tended not to turn out well for the other party. But I was in a bind here. So I'd make whatever reasonable deal I could. Then I'd get home.

"No deal," Prince Devyn said, calmly but not coldly. "You're going to have breakfast with me. There are dry clothes waiting for you in your room. You'll change, and then we'll eat."

I crossed my arms, determined not to give in to his manipulations. "I won't eat anything here," I said.

"And why's that?"

"Everyone knows that if you eat or drink anything in the realm of the fae, you end up trapped there." We might not learn a ton about the fae at Avalon Academy, but we'd learned that.

"You have fae blood," he said. "So that rule doesn't

apply to you. You can eat or drink anything you want here without being bound to remain in the Otherworld."

"Why should I believe you?"

"I'm a full fae," he said with a knowing smile. "I can't lie."

I nodded, since I'd known the answer before I'd asked. That was one of the few other things all supernaturals knew about the fae.

But at the same time, the entire world wobbled around me as realization finally hit. Because if he couldn't lie, it meant he was telling the truth. About *everything*.

Which meant Prince Devyn was my father.

10

SELENA

ONE OF PRINCE Devyn's slaves led me to "my room," where he left me in privacy to change into the outfit laid out for me.

The room itself was full of nature, with flowery vines growing down from the ceiling and along the walls. Otherwise, it was simply decorated with a single bed, nightstand, vanity, chair, and wardrobe. There were fresh rose petals laid out on the bed and a vase of flowers on the nightstand, as if they'd been expecting me.

Once I was alone, I searched for a way to escape. There was a big window off to the side, looking out to a field of daisies. I wasn't sure where I'd go in the field, but anywhere was better than being trapped with my biological faerie father who'd just *kidnapped me*.

If he wanted to get to know me, he could have done it in a civil way. A way I'd consented to. But kidnapping? I didn't care if he was related to me or not. That was *not* okay.

I ran to the window to unlatch it, but it was sealed shut. So I clawed at it harder. No matter how hard I tried to open it, the window wouldn't budge.

I lifted the chair next to the vanity and was about to try bashing it through the glass when Prince Devyn's voice rang through the door.

"The window is spelled," he said, loud enough for me to hear. "It shows an illusion instead of the city streets below. And you can't break through it. So please, put the chair down, Selena."

I spun to face the closed door, still holding tightly onto the chair. "You can see me?" I asked, looking around for cameras. There were none in plain sight, but that didn't mean they weren't hidden. I'd learned enough from the technology expert on Avalon—Thomas —to know that.

"No," he said. "And yes."

"What does that even mean?" How could the answer be no and yes? Faeries couldn't lie. But one of those had to be a lie. Right?

"I'll explain at breakfast," he said. "But please, put the chair down and change into the dress laid out for you.

Leave your current garb on the trunk at the end of the bed. The servants will take care of it. I'll see you in the dining room in a few minutes."

I heard his footsteps as he walked away, leaving me still holding onto the chair and wondering what kind of mess I'd been dragged into.

The outfit was a cloth, strappy maxi dress in a purple that matched my eyes. While it fit perfectly—as if tailor-made for me—it was impractical and totally unlike anything we wore on Avalon.

But when I looked at myself in the mirror, my reflection surprised me. Not because the dress looked good on me, which I had to admit, it did. But because my eyes looked brighter here, my skin more radiant, and my hair shinier. As if there were an otherworldly glow around me.

Goosebumps prickled on my arms at the reminder that I was half fae. It didn't feel real. None of this did. It felt like I was in some strange dream and that I'd wake up at any moment.

But since I was here, I wanted answers. Specifically, I wanted to know what kind of magic I could do as a fae —if I could do any at all.

Prince Devyn seemed willing to give me those answers. So it made sense to go out there, be as civil as possible, and talk to him.

I left Torrence's clothes on the trunk, like Prince Devyn had instructed, and ran my hand over the black top. It was too big on me in my true form, but the clothes reminded me of Torrence. They reminded me of home. I didn't want them taken away.

So I opened the wardrobe. It was full of dresses similar to this one. I placed the wet clothes on the bottom of the wardrobe, behind a lineup of colorful ballet flats.

Hopefully the clothes would still be there later.

Then I took another look at my reflection, took a deep breath, and headed out the door.

11

SELENA

THE GUARD WAITED outside my door and led me to the dining room.

Prince Devyn reclined on a chaise lounge in front of a table covered with an overflowing feast of fruits, meats, and cheeses. His shimmery wings cast a bright green glow behind him, and the tips of his ears poked out behind his shoulder-length hair.

"Selena." He looked me over approvingly and motioned to the lounge next to his. "Join me."

I was used to dining while sitting in a chair. But Prince Devyn reclined on his side, his forearm propped up on a pillow. So I walked over and situated myself in a similar position. It wasn't uncomfortable, but it felt strange. Especially because like Prince Devyn, I had my feet propped on the lounge as well.

He reached for his goblet and held it up. "I'm sure you have many questions, and we'll get to those in a moment," he said. "But first, a toast. Welcome to the Otherworld."

I reached for my goblet, trying to keep my hand from shaking. I couldn't say thank you, since according to legends, those words bound a person to a favor with the fae. I wasn't sure if the legend was true, but it was best not to risk it.

"I look forward to learning more about the Otherworld," I said, since it wasn't a lie. Then I raised my glass, and he clinked his with mine.

I took a quick sip of my drink, nearly spitting it out when sweet, honeyed wine hit my tongue.

"Is there a problem?" Prince Devyn raised an eyebrow in amusement.

I swallowed down the sweet wine. "You drink wine at breakfast?"

"Of course," he said. "But don't worry—it's not as strong as wine on Earth. You'll have to consume a lot more of it to feel its effects."

I frowned, since the conversation I was about to have with him was important. It wasn't in my best interest to get drunk, even if the wine was as weak as he claimed. "On Avalon, we only drink wine for special occasions, and only in the evenings," I said. "May I please have some water?"

"Absolutely not." He scoffed. "Water is for half-bloods. While you're technically a half-blood, you're also the daughter of a faerie prince and a witch. It's a combination that has never been seen before. So you'll be treated better than an average half-blood, and you will have wine."

From the snobby way he spoke, it was clear the request was not up for debate. Fine by me. I'd just drink as little wine as possible.

I wasn't going to waste my time fighting him for water when I could be getting what I *really* needed —information.

"Very well." I nodded and lifted the glass to sip from it again. I let the sweet liquid brush my lips, although I only pretended to drink.

"Octavius. Seneca," Devyn said, looking to the slaves standing at the door. "Please leave my daughter and I to dine in private."

The two men bowed their heads in tandem and saw themselves out, closing the door behind them.

Devyn reached for a bunch of grapes, plucked one from it, and popped it in his mouth. "I'm sure you have many questions," he said, watching me curiously.

That was the understatement of the century.

I wasn't that hungry, since I'd just had dinner and dessert. But I reached for a bit of cheese and chewed on it as I wracked my mind to figure out where to start. "You say you're my father," I said after swallowing the cheese. "But why didn't I know about you until now?"

"That wasn't my decision." He looked at me sadly. "I wanted you to live here with me. It was part of the agreement I made with your mother."

"Agreement?" The word tasted so sour on my tongue that I took a tiny sip of the honeyed wine to wash it away.

"Almost seventeen years ago, Camelia Conrad sought me out to make a bargain," he said. "She agreed to two things. Firstly, to give me her first-born child. Secondly, to let me take her virginity. The latter resulted in your conception."

"You knew." Something about the confident way he spoke made me sure of it. "You knew that by taking her virginity that night, you'd get her pregnant."

"I did."

"But how—"

"More on that later," he cut me off. "Because according to the deal, I was supposed to have you as well. But your mother hid you away on Avalon, knowing it was the only place on Earth my kind couldn't track you or contact you. As you know, she died shortly after giving birth to you. What you don't know is that before handing you over to the care of your adoptive parents, she forced them to enter into a blood oath. She made them promise they'd never tell you of your fae heritage, and never allow you to leave Avalon."

My head spun as I took in the information. What he'd just told me was a huge relief. My parents were the most honest, loving people I knew. Of course they wouldn't have kept something so huge from me of their own free will.

"But my birth mother was dying," I said. "Why would my parents agree to the blood oath?"

"Camelia was holding you," he said. "She threatened to take your life if they didn't agree to the oath."

I shuddered at the awfulness of what he'd said. I knew my birth mother had done terrible things. But until now, I hadn't known she'd stoop to *that*.

If I wasn't hungry before, I certainly wasn't hungry now. I placed the remainder of the piece of cheese on the plate in front of me.

"Then Camelia used her Final Spell to bind your faerie magic," he said. "To hide it from others and make it impossible for you to access."

In that moment, everything made a surprising amount of sense. "My magic," I repeated, feeling it crackle inside of me and flare to life as I spoke of it, like a storm within me. I looked at my hand, as if I could will it to the surface. But as always, nothing happened. "It's real."

"Of course it's real," he said, as if I were crazy for thinking otherwise. "Your magic is woven into your soul. Even your mother couldn't take it away from you. But it's repressed. Bound. Even though it's in you, you can't utilize it."

"Can you unbind it?" Hope knotted in my chest, and I held my breath in anticipation.

If Prince Devyn could unbind my magic, then perhaps being brought here wasn't such a terrible thing, after all.

"No," he said, and my hope deflated.

"Why not?" I asked. "Isn't fae magic stronger than witch magic?"

"It's much stronger," he said. "But not even a fae can reverse a witch's Final Spell."

"How do you know?" I asked. "Can't you just try?"

"It won't work."

As if I'd accept defeat that easily. "You can't know that."

"Yes, I can," he said. "I know every possible outcome of every possible situation. Because I—like all royal fae —have a special gift. And my gift is omniscient sight."

12

SELENA

"So you can see the future?"

A prophetess lived on Avalon—a gifted vampire named Skylar Danvers. She saw the future in tarot cards. So this wasn't something I was unfamiliar with.

"I don't just see *the* future," he said. "I see *all* futures."

"What do you mean?"

"You know a prophetess from Avalon," he said. "Skylar Danvers."

I blinked, stunned. "Did you just read my mind?"

"No." He chuckled. "I'm not telepathic."

"Then how did you know I was thinking about her?"

"That was luck," he said. "It was highly probable that you'd think of the prophetess you know at the mention of my gift."

I nodded, since it made sense. "Yes," I said, wanting to get back to the point. "I know Skylar."

"She can see the most likely future at that point in time," he said. "But that's all she sees when she looks into her tarot cards. *One* future. The one most likely to happen. That one future can change, so it's not a given that what she sees in the cards will play out in reality. But my gift—omniscient sight—allows me to see more than just one future. I can see all futures. Every possible one of them. A complicated, interwoven web, with some strands stronger and more likely to occur than others."

"Wow," I said. "That must be… confusing."

"It can be." He gave me a pained smile. "Oftentimes, my ability is more of a curse than a gift. Knowing every possible way the future can pan out tends to take the joy out of living." He sounded so sad, and for a split second, I felt bad for him.

"I'm sorry," I said, and then I chewed on a fig, at a loss for what else to say.

"Don't be," he said. "I do my best to use my gift for good. Although I learned centuries ago that sharing what I see with others leads to anxiety regarding bad scenarios, and unwanted changes in good scenarios that then change them into bad scenarios. So I almost always keep what I see to myself. But I promise you, Selena, there's no possible future in which I'm able to remove the binding spell your birth mother placed on you. Trying would only lead to wasted time and disappointment."

"*You* can't remove the binding spell," I said, remembering to pay attention to the nuances of what he said. While faeries couldn't lie, they were talented at talking around the truth. "But is there another fae that can?"

"Your mother's Final Spell was strong," he said. "No fae can remove it."

"So why bring me here at all?" I asked. "I have no witch magic, and I can't access my fae magic. I'm useless."

"You couldn't be more wrong," he said. "You're far from useless."

"So there's a reason you brought me here." I figured there had to be, given his omniscient sight. He hadn't gone to this much trouble to kidnap me so I could scrub floors and toilets, or whatever the half-blood slaves did around here.

Or maybe he had. Maybe he just wanted to finish the deal he'd made with my birth mother all those years ago.

"You look troubled," he observed. "What's on your mind?"

"Shouldn't you already know that?" I was goading him. But I didn't care.

"Like I said, I'm not telepathic." He popped another

grape into his mouth and watched me patiently. From his relaxed manner, it seemed like he'd wait all day.

So I might as well be out with it.

"You didn't bring me here to be a slave, right? Because I'm not exactly slave material." That was an understatement, given the way I'd been raised. "You'll get a far better deal going to my parents and making a bargain with them in exchange for my safe passage back to Avalon."

"First of all, the half-bloods aren't slaves," he said. "They're servants."

"What's the difference?" Both sounded bad to me.

"Servants are paid. Slaves are not."

"Oh," I said, since he was right. Being a slave sounded worse than a servant. Although I had a feeling from the few servants I'd seen that they weren't paid much.

"I didn't bring you here to be a servant," he said. "You're far more important than that." He leaned forward, a chilling glint in his eyes as he fixated his violet gaze on mine. "I brought you here to nominate you to play in this year's Faerie Games."

13

SELENA

HE SPOKE of the Faerie Games like it was supposed to mean something to me.

It didn't.

"What are the Faerie Games?" I asked once it became apparent that he was waiting for me to speak next.

"Just something us fae do every year," he said casually. "To entertain ourselves and the gods."

My magic crackled, like a warning. "Which gods?" I asked, leaning closer to the edge of my lounge. I'd learned enough in school to know he could be talking about any variety of gods. They all existed, in some way or another. Although they rarely—if ever—showed themselves.

"The only ones that matter," he said. "At least, the only ones that matter here in the Otherworld, where they've reigned for over fifteen hundred years. The Roman gods."

"Whoa." I didn't know what I'd been expecting, but it certainly hadn't been that. "You mean Zeus and Poseidon and Hades and all of them?"

"Those are the Greek gods." He made a face, as if the mix-up appalled him. "At least, that's what the Greeks called them. In the Otherworld, we pay homage to the greatest civilization to ever live on Earth—the Roman Empire. We refer to the gods by their true Roman names. The ones you mentioned are Jupiter, Neptune, and Pluto, in that order."

"Right," I said, remembering this from Ancient Magical History 101. "Same gods, different names. Got it."

"They're not the same gods." Again, Prince Devyn looked at me as if what I'd said was highly offensive. "The Roman gods are stronger, smarter, and more focused than their Greek counterparts. They're worthy of being worshipped by the greatest civilization to ever live on Earth. But after the Roman Empire fell—since all human civilizations eventually fall, even the most powerful ones—the gods relocated to the only other place where they were still appreciated and worshipped. The Otherworld."

"The gods are actually here?" I asked. "The fae have interacted with them?"

"They're actually here," he said. "But they mostly keep to themselves. The one time a year we interact with them is during the Faerie Games. Three of them actively show themselves during the Games. Bacchus, the god of wine and celebrations, hosts the Games. Vesta, the goddess of the home, lives in the villa with the players to watch over and help them. And Juno, the queen of the gods, makes the rules and crowns the winner."

"What about the other gods?" I asked.

"The eleven most powerful gods in the pantheon can pick a half-blood player to represent them in the Games," he said. "Although they only choose a player if they feel one of the nominees is worthy to represent them. Otherwise, they'll sit out. Usually six to eight players are chosen each year."

"And you want to nominate me to be one of those players."

"Yes." His eyes gleamed. "Every year, each faerie prince and princess can nominate one player for the Games. If selected for the Games, the half-blood nominee is gifted with magic from the god that chose them. It's a great honor to be chosen to represent a god in the Games."

"Back up." I held up a hand, taking in what he'd said. "You mean if I'm nominated by a god, I'll have magic?"

"You will," he confirmed. "Powerful magic rivaling that of a full-blooded fae."

I smiled, liking the idea of being nominated for these Games more and more. "So if I'm chosen by a god, I play in the Faerie Games," I said. "Then, once the Games are over, I'll be free to go home?"

"The winner of the Games earns his or her freedom and is no longer a half-blood servant," he said. "So, yes. If you win the Games, you'll be free to leave the Otherworld, if that's what you still wish to do."

"And if I don't win the Games?" I watched him carefully, expecting some kind of catch.

"If you don't win, you'll have no future to bargain for," he said. "Because you'll be dead."

14

SELENA

I SHOT up into a sitting position, looking at him in horror. "What do you mean?" I asked, even though what he meant was clear. I just needed a few seconds to process it. "Are you saying that the Faerie Games are played to the death? Like some kind of barbaric gladiator game?"

"Precisely." He pursed his lips. "Although the Faerie Games aren't barbaric."

"You're having people fight to the death—for *entertainment*," I said. "That sounds pretty barbaric to me."

"It's entertaining," he said. "But it's also necessary. After all, we can't have too many half-bloods gifted with powers from the gods as free citizens in the Otherworld. That would upset the balance of our community. So each year, the chosen players compete in the Games, and the winner earns his or her freedom. The winner is also provided a generous stipend for life. It's a wonderful opportunity. Most half-bloods are thrilled to be chosen, or even nominated."

I shook my head, horror racing through my body as I looked at him. This was so twisted.

"And if I don't want to be nominated?" I asked, tension edging in my tone.

"You don't have a choice," he said. "I *will* be nominating you for this year's Faerie Games. If a god chooses you, you will play. And hopefully you will win."

"No." I glared at him, anger sparking under my skin. He couldn't force me to do this. He couldn't keep me here.

I wanted to go home. To do that, I needed one of those portal tokens in his pocket. I'd seen him put them there. If I could just get to one...

I leaped forward, a hand stretched out to reach into his pocket and steal a token.

He waved his hand and a burst of green magic flew at me, throwing me back into my seat. I tried to move, but it was no use. I was stuck.

"What did you do to me?" I asked, all but feral with anger now. My magic crackled inside of me. But like always, no matter how angry I got, my magic refused to release.

"You're not strong enough to fight fae magic." He looked at me like I was a lost puppy. "Relax, Selena. I'm your father. I have your best interests at heart."

"Prince Jacen Pearce of Avalon is my father," I said. "Not you."

"I am your blood." He remained frustratingly calm as I continued to push against his magical hold on me. "Nothing will ever change that."

"Fine." I stilled and gave up on fighting his magic, since my efforts were failing. "If you truly care about my best interests, then send me home. If you send me home now, I promise I won't have the Nephilim army of Avalon come after you to punish you for kidnapping. Which they *will* do, if you don't cooperate."

"Resorting to threats now, are we?"

"It's not a threat," I said. "It's a promise."

"Your Nephilim army is no threat against the fae." He released me from his magical hold, as if proving his point.

"The Nephilim army is the most powerful army in the world." I sat back up, flexing my fingers to confirm I could move again. "They're a threat to everyone. Don't underestimate them."

"I'm not underestimating anyone," he said. "I'm simply stating the truth. Or have you already forgotten that I can see all possible futures?"

He was right. I'd gotten so angry about the Faerie Games that I hadn't taken that piece of information into account.

But I wouldn't give him the satisfaction of admitting it.

"You claim you want what's best for me," I repeated, and he nodded. "Does that mean that in all possible futures, I'll win the Faerie Games if I'm chosen to play? Is that why you want to nominate me?"

"I already told you." He sighed and massaged his temple. "I don't like to tell anyone what I've seen of the future. It never ends well."

I narrowed my eyes at him. "You just avoided answering my question."

"I did," he said, dropping his hand back to his side. "But you need to trust me, and trust my gift. The future will always be a better place if you're nominated for the Games than if you're not. If I don't nominate you tomorrow—"

"The nominations are *tomorrow*?"

"They are," he said. "And the Games start immediately afterward."

Crap. That didn't leave me a lot of time to talk my way out of this, or for my parents to rescue me.

Panic squeezed my lungs.

I never should have drunk Torrence's transformation potion.

"I'm not ready," I said, desperate now. "At least give me time to get ready. You said the Games happen every year. Can't you wait to nominate me until next year's Games?"

By then, hopefully I'd have figured out a way to hightail it out of there.

"That's not an option," he said. "I'll be nominating you tomorrow."

"Is there anything I can do or say to change your mind?" It sounded pathetic when spoken out loud. But since he couldn't lie, I needed to know the answer.

"No," he said, and with that single word, I felt my fate seal into place. "But I will tell you this, and nothing more. Trust yourself and your instincts. Do that, and you'll have the best chance at winning the Games."

15

TORRENCE

NOT BEING able to use my powers in front of anyone while I was pretending to be Selena was ridiculously hard. But I managed.

Barely.

I was playing a game of soccer—witches against shifters—when the Earth Angel teleported into the center of the field. She caught the ball right after I'd given it a hard kick in the air, stopping it from making a goal.

Everyone stopped playing at the sight of her.

She looked at me oddly, and I immediately knew why. Selena didn't like sports, let alone play them for fun. Yet there I was, playing front and center, having a total blast.

Oops.

The Earth Angel tossed the ball toward the nearest person—the hot mage, Reed.

He caught it easily.

"Selena," the Earth Angel said, looking straight at me with her golden eyes. Even though she was my best friend's mom, she still intimidated me. Angels and Nephilim tended to have that effect on people. "I need to speak with you. Come with me." She walked over to me and held her hands out.

I looked at her hands strangely and almost asked where we were going. Then I remembered—since Selena had no magic, she couldn't teleport herself. It usually didn't matter on Avalon, since we were discouraged from teleporting unless absolutely necessary. It was expected that we save our magic, and get the exercise.

Whatever was going on, it was clearly important.

Had Selena and I been caught? I hoped not. She'd never forgive me. Well, she *would* forgive me—she always did. But it was going to take a lot of groveling.

"All right," I said, reaching out to take the Earth Angel's hands.

She teleported us off the soccer field and into the private quarters she shared with Prince Jacen.

Selena's dad was pacing around so much that he could have worn down the Turkish rug. He stilled when we arrived and looked at me, worry shining in his strange silver eyes.

The Earth Angel was by his side in an instant. Now that her guard wasn't up, I saw that she was worried, too.

That was somewhat good, right? If they'd found out about the swap, they'd be *angry*. Not worried.

This had to be about something else. Something totally unrelated to Selena out there in California pretending to be me.

"There's no easy way to say this, and we wanted you to hear it from us first," Jacen started. "So I'm just going to get on with it. Torrence is missing."

I looked back and forth between them in shock. This had to be a joke.

But their solemn expressions remained the same.

"What do you mean, she's *missing*?" I finally managed to say.

"Her mom called soon after waking up this morning," the Earth Angel said. "She went to wake Torrence up for breakfast, and she was gone. At first she thought perhaps Torrence had come back to Avalon early without saying good-bye, but her stuff was still in her room. And Torrence is nowhere to be found on Avalon."

"She can't just be gone," I sputtered, panic coursing through me. "Can't my mo—" I almost said my mom, but stopped myself. "Can't Amber do a tracking spell to find her?"

"She tried." Pity shined in the Earth Angel's golden eyes. "The spell found nothing."

I swallowed, overrun with so much horror that I needed to sit down in one of the armchairs surrounding the fireplace. Because if my mom couldn't track her, that meant one of two things.

Either someone was using a cloaking spell to keep her location hidden.

Or she was dead.

But no. That wasn't right.

Because they were searching for *me*. Tracking spells weren't fooled by transformation potion. It was impossible to locate Avalon, let alone track anyone on the island. Since I'd been on Avalon this entire time, of course the tracking spells resulted in nothing.

They needed to be searching for *Selena*.

Which meant I needed to tell her parents the truth.

"I think you guys should sit down." I held onto the arms of the chair, bracing myself for whatever was to come. "Because I have something important to tell you. And you're not going to like it."

TORRENCE

I WAS RIGHT.

Selena's parents were pissed off.

They didn't even yell at me, which was the scariest part. They just looked at each other in fear and walked into the bedroom of their quarters, telling me to stay where I was before slamming the door shut.

There must have been a sound barrier spell around their bedroom, because I couldn't hear a word they said in there. I chewed on my thumbnails as I waited. That was a habit of *mine*, not Selena's. But now that the cat was out of the bag, there was no need to hide my habits anymore.

Finally, after what felt like forever, Prince Jacen and the Earth Angel emerged from their room. But now, the three mages—Dahlia, Violet, and Iris—were with them.

As always, the mages wore floor-length medieval gowns. They were the only ones on Avalon who dressed formally every day. The rest of us preferred casual, comfortable clothes. Even the Earth Angel and Prince Jacen.

"Torrence," Dahlia said, looking me over uneasily. "I trust you created an antidote pill?"

"Of course I did." Witchcraft 101 said to *always* create antidote pills for every potion created.

"Fetch it, bring it back here, and take it," she said. "As quickly as possible. It'll be best for everyone present to have you in this conversation in your true form."

I teleported into the manor house, rushed inside the female witch dormitory, and reached into the underside of my pillowcase. The antidote pill was just where I'd left it.

Pill in hand, I teleported back into Prince Jacen and the Earth Angel's quarters. Well, I *tried* teleporting back inside. Just like in the manor house, there was a privacy barrier spell around their quarters. So I ended up outside their door.

I knocked and was ushered back inside by Dahlia.

"You got it?" she asked.

I opened my palm, showing her the red antidote pill. Then I popped it in my mouth and chewed.

Like all antidote pills, it was chalky and hard to swallow. But I forced it down. I watched my hands shimmer in front of me, and seconds later, I was back in my true form. My black Avalon Academy jumpsuit changed shape with me.

The Earth Angel looked at me, her golden eyes harsh with anger. "Take a seat," she said, motioning to the sitting area in front of the fireplace.

I situated myself in one of the armchairs again. The three mages all sat in the larger sofa together, and Prince Jacen and the Earth Angel took the loveseat across from me.

"Selena's life is in danger with every passing second, so we don't have much time," the Earth Angel began. "Bella's been informed about the situation and is doing a tracking spell to find her. Because of a blood oath that was made, Jacen, Dahlia, Violet, and I cannot tell you why Selena's in danger."

"What kind of blood oath?" I asked, looking suspiciously between all of them.

"One that was made on the night of Selena's birth," Iris said. She sat closest to me, and as always, she wore a green gown. "But I wasn't in the room when the blood oath was made. Thus, I'm not bound to it."

"So you can tell me what it is?"

"I don't know all the details, as they've been withheld

from me because of the blood oath," she began. "But over the years, I've pieced things together and realized what must have happened on my own."

"Selena's biological mother went into labor on the night of Prince Jacen and the Earth Angel's wedding," I said what everyone already knew. "She died giving birth and entrusted Selena to Prince Jacen and the Earth Angel's care. What else is there to know?"

From the pained look on the faces of everyone in the room with me, I guessed there was a *lot* more to know.

"Selena's biological mother—Camelia—was only permitted to live on Avalon because she was pregnant and her baby needed to be kept safe," Iris started. "You see, she'd made a deal with the fae. She'd promised them her firstborn child. But she didn't want them to have that child. So there was only one place she could go where the fae couldn't find her."

"Avalon," I said.

"Correct." Iris nodded. "She died giving birth to Selena and entrusted her to Prince Jacen and the Earth Angel's care, as is public knowledge. But there are… peculiarities with Selena's magic."

"Selena doesn't have any magic," I said. "She *wants* to have it, and she tries, but…" I paused and shrugged. Because as much as I wanted Selena to learn to harness the magic she said she felt, the fact that she still hadn't managed even the simplest spell was a bad sign.

I'd always figured that her biological father must have barely carried any witch genes at all.

"She *does* have magic," Iris said. "But the descriptions she gives of the magic she feels inside of her isn't witch magic. It's faerie magic."

"Selena's biological parents are witches," I said. "How can she have faerie magic?"

"Because Selena's biological father isn't a witch," she said. "He's a faerie."

I looked at her in shock. This couldn't be true. It didn't add up.

"When Camelia went to the crossroads to make a deal with the fae, she didn't only promise her first born," Iris continued. "She also conceived a child with the fae who made the deal with her."

"But faeries are stronger than witches *and* mages," I said. "So if Selena's half fae, why can't she do magic?"

"I'm getting to that part." Iris held out her hands, as if she were telling me to stop talking and start listening. "You see, all of us in this room knew the truth of Selena's heritage. But after Selena's birth, none of them would talk about it. It didn't take me long to realize why. When they were all in Camelia's chambers helping Camelia give birth, Camelia must have bound them to an oath of silence. But she must have been so feverish with blood loss that she didn't remember there was one more person who knew the truth of Selena's parentage, who wasn't in that room with them. Me." She squared her shoulders, smiling proudly.

"Why weren't you in the room with them that night?" I asked.

"Camelia went into labor in the middle of Prince Jacen and the Earth Angel's wedding," she explained. "Someone had to oversee the ending of the celebration and keep the rest of the citizens of Avalon in line and happy. The job was mine."

"So you weren't bound to the blood oath," I said, and she nodded. "So why didn't you tell Selena the truth? Why keep this from her for all those years? Do you know how much she'd kill to know she has magic?"

"I didn't tell her because she doesn't have magic," she said sadly. "At least, not magic she can access."

"What do you mean?"

"It took me a while to figure out, but after a few years of observing Selena as she grew up, I realized what must have happened," she said. "Camelia knew she was dying. As you know, a witch can perform extraordinarily strong magic if they put their entire force behind it, although it will cost them their lives."

"A Final Spell." I stared at her in shock.

Final Spells tended to be cast in one of two situations. Either an extreme sacrifice, or when a witch knew they were about to die.

My mouth dropped open as I put the pieces together. "Camelia used her Final Spell on Selena."

17

TORRENCE

"Yes." Iris nodded. "Camelia used her Final Spell to bind Selena's faerie magic. I tried my hardest to figure out how to unbind it, but nothing worked. Selena will never be able to access her faerie magic. I feared telling her would only cause her frustration—and potential danger if she tried to get her faerie magic unbound on her own. So I said nothing."

"That wasn't your decision to make." I glared at her, livid on my best friend's behalf. "Selena has a right to know what she is."

"This is a discussion best suited for another time," the Earth Angel said, bringing the focus back to her and Prince Jacen. "Because my daughter is out there right now, and faeries are after her to take her to the Other-world. You know she's prohibited from leaving the island." Her golden eyes were as harsh as ever, and I shrank in my seat. "What were you thinking, giving her that transformation potion and letting her leave Avalon?"

"I was thinking that she's never been allowed off Avalon, and that she should be able to see a bit of the world beyond this small island," I said, my tone rising with frustration. "How was I supposed to know the fae were after her?"

Prince Jacen's stern gaze fixated on mine. "It wasn't your job to question our rules," he said. "But you thought you knew better. You defied us."

"I thought she wasn't allowed off Avalon because demons would be after her for being your daughter!" I said. "I thought that if she took the transformation potion and went as *me,* it wouldn't matter. I leave Avalon every weekend. I didn't think—"

"You didn't think the rules mattered," he said. "You didn't consider that prohibiting Selena from leaving Avalon was absolutely necessary. You thought you knew better than we did."

"I did." I lowered my eyes, ashamed. "I'm sorry. I didn't realize..." I trailed off, unable to think of anything to say that would be sufficient enough of an apology.

Because Prince Jacen was right. I'd given Selena that transformation potion because I thought the rule that she couldn't leave Avalon was stupid. I didn't think anything bad would happen to her in LA, especially with her disguised as me.

Now the fae might have taken her to the Otherworld.

"This is all my fault." Tears filled my eyes as I looked back up at Prince Jacen and the Earth Angel.

"It's not *all* your fault," the Earth Angel said. "You didn't force Selena to drink that transformation potion and go to LA. She did that on her own. She should have said no. Maybe, if we'd allowed Iris to tell her the truth of her heritage..."

Prince Jacen placed his hand lovingly on hers, stopping her from continuing. "We can't think like that," he said. "We both know our daughter. She's curious. If she knew the truth of her heritage, she would have eventually left to seek answers on her own."

"Maybe." The Earth Angel sighed, worry shining in her eyes. "Maybe not. But at least if she'd done that, she would have been protected and prepared. Now she's out there on her own."

A sitting duck for the fae to snatch up and abduct to the Otherworld.

Hollowness twisted in my gut. Selena was out there alone because of me. The Earth Angel might be too nice to say it, but it was true.

This was my fault.

"Maybe the fae didn't take her," I said, my voice strained as I spoke. "Maybe she went to the ocean by herself or something. Maybe she'll come back in an hour or so and she'll be perfectly fine."

I wanted it to be true.

But as I said it, I didn't believe it.

"Bella's doing a tracking spell to locate her," the Earth Angel reminded me. "She'll report back immediately once she has the results."

We sat there for a few agonizingly silent minutes waiting for Aunt Bella to return. I wanted to say something to help, but there was nothing to say. Instead, I prayed to every god out there that Selena would be okay.

Eventually, there was a knock on the door.

The Earth Angel stood up and let Aunt Bella inside.

From the grim expression on my aunt's face, I knew she didn't come bearing good news.

"Well?" The Earth Angel looked at her hopefully.

Always confident, Aunt Bella held her head high. "My tracking spell couldn't find Selena," she said. "I'm sorry."

The world swirled around me. Because this meant one of three things.

Selena was on Earth, but wearing a cloaking ring to hide her location.

Selena was dead.

Or Selena had been taken by the fae to the Otherworld.

Prince Jacen looked at the Earth Angel, determination flaring in his silver eyes. "I'll go to the crossroads tonight," he said. "I'll make a deal with the fae to get her back."

"What if it's too late?" The Earth Angel shivered, clearly not wanting to share the possibilities running through her mind.

"The fae went to great lengths to find her," Prince Jacen said, always confident under pressure. "They're not going to harm her." He sounded so convincing that I believed him. "And the fae are always open to deals. There *will* be something they want. And I'll give them anything in return for our daughter's safety."

The Earth Angel nodded, looking too shocked to speak any more.

"What can I do to help?" I asked, twisting my fingers in my lap.

"You've done enough as it is," Prince Jacen said sharply. "Go to your mother and tell her you're safe. Then return to school tomorrow. Tell no one what you learned about Selena's true heritage, as they'll hear it from us first, when the time is right. We'll handle the rest."

From the way he was looking at me, I knew it wasn't up for debate.

"I really am sorry," I said. "If you need anything—"

"Just go," the Earth Angel said. "Your mother is worried sick. She'll be glad to hear you're okay."

From the pain in her voice, I knew she was thinking about how much she wanted to know Selena was okay, too. My heart ached for her. And for Selena, too.

But they wanted me gone, so I teleported out. Of course I'd do as they'd asked and tell my mom I was okay.

But I wasn't going to sit back and do nothing after that.

Because I'd gotten Selena into this mess.

And I intended to help get her out of it.

18

SELENA

I BARELY SLEPT THAT NIGHT.

How was I supposed to sleep in the nature-filled child's room Prince Devyn had prepared for me, knowing that he was nominating me for a competition that would likely send me to my death?

His servants had delivered a platter of passion fruit late in the evening, claiming it would help me sleep. The exotic pink fruits were cut in half and served with a small spoon. But I didn't trust that they weren't drugged. And because the servants were half-bloods and not full fae, they were capable of lying. So the fruit remained on my vanity, untouched, when the sun rose the next morning.

At least, I assumed that the sun rising over the ocean

in my magical mirage window meant that the sun was rising in the real outside world, too.

I was finally starting to drift asleep when someone knocked on my door, entering without waiting for me to tell them to come in. A woman with long, wavy black hair and stunning pale green eyes. She wore a gown that matched her eyes, with gold swirls stitched within it. Her sparkly wings were bright yellow and she had pointed ears that poked out of her hair. She was a full fae.

"Who are you?" I clutched my comforter to my chest, instantly going on the defense at the sight of one of *them* in my room.

"I'm Nessa," she said. "Prince Devyn asked me to get you ready for the nomination ceremony today."

"Are you his girlfriend or something?" I didn't see a ring on her finger, although I supposed faeries might not have that same custom.

"No." She laughed, and the sound was melodic, like a bubbling stream. "Prince Devyn and I are old friends. We go back centuries."

I looked her up and down. She didn't look a day older than twenty-four. I was used to being around immortals, since everyone was immortal while living on Avalon. But it was rare to encounter ones that had been around for so many years.

"And you're okay that he's nominating me—his own *daughter*—for these Faerie Games?" The word daughter felt sour on my tongue, since I'd never consider Prince Devyn to be my father.

Serenity flicked across her features. "Devyn does everything for a reason," she said. "I've learned not to question him. He's helped me more times than I care to admit. Which is why I'm doing him the favor of helping you get ready for the ceremony."

"I don't need help." I threw off my comforter and swung my legs off the bed. "I can get ready myself."

"Don't be silly." She laughed again. "You know nothing of our culture and of our ceremonies. You don't want the general public to dislike you on sight for breaking protocol."

"Why not?" I didn't care what the general faerie public thought of me. All I wanted was to go home.

"Having their favor can be helpful in the Games," she said. "Everything you do from the moment you appear at the nomination ceremony until the end of your time in the Games will be watched and judged by everyone living in the citadel. The more popular you are with the people, the more likely the Games will go in your favor. Understood?"

From the conniving way she looked at me, I understood, all right.

The Faerie Games were rigged.

If the approval of the public meant they could be rigged in my favor, then yes—I wanted the approval of the public. Because above all else, I wanted to live.

"Understood." I kept my gaze locked on hers, hoping to get across the message that even though she was a full fae and I was a mere half-blood with no powers, I wouldn't be intimidated by her. "Let's get me ready for this ceremony."

Nessa dressed me in a simple purple maxi dress similar to the one I wore yesterday. Unlike hers, it didn't have any stitching on it. She explained it was because only faeries were allowed decorative elements on their clothing. Half-bloods could only wear plain, solid colored clothes.

Half-bloods also weren't permitted to wear makeup, so that eliminated a lot of time from getting ready. And finally, half-blood females were all required to wear our hair up and out of our face. So Nessa styled my hair in a slick high ponytail, although she curled it at the ends and wrapped a piece of hair around the band to make it more elegant.

One of the male servants came in while she was doing my hair to deliver me a breakfast platter of bread and cheese. I didn't want to eat their food, but I was starving. And it wouldn't do me any good to go into this nomination ceremony hungry.

So I devoured the entire thing.

"Now, for the real reason Prince Devyn sent me here," Nessa said, wrapping a hand around the top of my arm. Her grip was firm, and it warmed up, bright yellow magic glowing around her hand. The magic sank into my skin, making my entire arm tingle.

When she removed her hand, a red band was wrapped around my arm. I recognized the band—I'd seen identical ones on the two servants yesterday.

"What's that for?" I asked.

"All half-bloods are given this tattoo at birth," she said. "It has ink made of fae blood, which makes it so half-bloods can never use their magic against the fae, or hurt our kind in any way."

"You just gave me a tattoo?" I recoiled and looked down at the red band in horror. I had nothing against tattoos in general, but if something was going to be inked on me for life, I wanted to choose what it was. Not have it forced upon me.

"No." She laughed again, as if I were the most

amusing person she'd come across in ages. "The process for the tattoo takes more time, and it's rather agonizing. That's why we give it to half-bloods when they're infants—so they won't remember being inked. But you have no magic, so you have no need for a real tattoo. This one is simply an illusion. I'm one of the best illusionists in the Otherworld." She smiled and waved her hand in the air, yellow magic shooting out of her hand and toward my window. Within a second, the image outside transformed from the beach we'd been looking at all morning to a fairytale castle on a hill. "See?"

Rage boiled in my chest as I stared down at the tattoo. "So the half-bloods *are* slaves," I said darkly.

"Not slaves." She raised a hand to her chest in horror. "They're servants. They're paid a fair wage for their work."

It was the same thing Prince Devyn had said.

"They might be paid wages," I said. "But these tattoos keep them in chains. That makes them slaves."

"The tattoos keep the fae protected." She stuck her nose in the air, clearly not in the mood for a debate about this. "But your opinion about the tattoos is irrelevant. You have something more important to worry about right now. The Faerie Games."

As if I needed the reminder. The Games had been weighing on me all night.

But as much as I hated the thought of the half-bloods being kept in magical chains, there was nothing I could do about the tattoos. So Nessa was right. I needed to remain focused on the Games.

"Why bother with the illusion of a tattoo for me at all?" I asked. "I don't have any magic. I'm not a threat."

"You're definitely not a threat." The way she said it made me feel lower than dirt. "But like I said at first, you want the approval of the public. Magic or not, they wouldn't be trustful of a half-blood nominee without a tattoo. Thus, the illusion." She looked back down at the fake tattoo she'd given me and beamed. "No one will know the difference between this and the real thing."

She stepped back and looked me over, taking her time as she checked for imperfections.

I felt like a bug under a microscope.

"You've inherited your father's good looks," she said. "That'll be advantageous for you in the Games."

I doubted my looks mattered in a faerie gladiator battle to the death. But she was still just standing there, staring at me. Like she was waiting for me to say something.

She probably wanted me to thank her, which would force me into owing her a favor. No way was I falling for that.

"Any advantage I might have is a welcome one." I

gave her a tight smile that I hoped got across the message that I wouldn't fall for her tricks.

She nodded in approval and looked at me with what might have been respect. "Well, it seems my work here is done," she said. "Let's send you off to the nomination ceremony."

19

SELENA

NESSA LED me down spiral steps in the back of the house that ended in a place that looked like a mix of a barn and a garage.

There was a round chariot in the center that reminded me of the one Cinderella had taken to the royal ball. Made of frosted glass, it had massive ornate wheels and white flowers piled on top that wound down along the windows. A half-blood servant sat in the driver's seat, ready to go.

But the carriage wasn't the most magnificent thing in the garage. Because connected to the front of the carriage was a majestic white horse with shimmery feather wings.

I was taking in the beauty of the winged horse when

someone opened the chariot door from within and poked his blond head out.

Prince Devyn.

"Get in," he commanded. "We don't have all day."

The half-blood guards stood in front of the door leading back to the house. And I had known that Prince Devyn wouldn't hesitate to use his magic on me again. So I did as he asked and stepped into the carriage.

The vehicle, while pretty, was also confining. It felt like sitting inside a Christmas ornament.

The gates opened, and the horse trotted out of the garage and onto the cobblestone street. The moment we were outside, the horse opened its wings and lifted the carriage into the air. My stomach swooped, and I pressed a hand against the frosted glass, looking down at the sprawling city below.

Full of elegant marble buildings, the city looked like the drawings in my history books of Ancient Rome. But unlike those drawings, vines and flowers decorated the sides of these buildings, making it uniquely fae. Among the buildings, I recognized the Coliseum in the center. It looked just like the one in Rome, although this one wasn't in ruins, and it was decorated with greenery.

"Our capital city, Augustus," Devyn said. "Beautiful, isn't it?"

"It is," I agreed, and then stared at him straight on. "If

I wasn't being held as a captive, perhaps I'd enjoy my time here."

"I wish you wouldn't look at it that way," he said. "You should feel at peace here. The Otherworld is your home."

I sat back and sighed, not wanting to have this conversation again.

We spent the remainder of the forty-five-minute flight in silence.

It was a relief to us both when the horse descended toward the ground.

Like it had been since getting outside the city boundary, the scenery around us was full of bright green hills. But as we came across the final crest, I saw a field where other carriages and winged horses were lined up in neat rows.

A faerie parking lot.

The carriages were all round, although the colors, wheels, and flowers decorating them varied greatly. Not one of them looked the same.

A half-blood directed us into a space. Once stopped, our driver got up and opened the door for us, ushering us out of the carriage. A handful of other fae with their half-blood nominees were also exiting their carriages, although judging by the full field, most everyone had arrived by now.

"The Stone of Destiny isn't far from here," Prince Devyn said, leading the way toward the nearest hill.

I kept up behind him. "What's the Stone of Destiny?" I asked.

"It's the location of the nomination ceremony," he said. "Where you'll be presented to the gods, and they'll decide your fate."

20

SELENA

THE STONE of Destiny was a tall, vertical stone about twenty feet high that sat at the top of a nearby hill. Faeries and their half-blood nominees lined up around it, starting near the top and spiraling down the hill. There must have been nearly a hundred pairs of us in all.

All the half-bloods looked either my age or slightly older, so I assumed there was an age cutoff for nominations. And most of them wore rings similar to Julian's.

"What do those rings mean?" I asked Devyn, glancing at the ring on the finger of the girl in front of me.

"They're promise rings," he said. "Given to a half-blood from a faerie prince or princess, as an agreement to nominate them for the Games."

Each faerie stood next to their half-blood, so it was

clear who they were nominating. They might as well have given us collars and leashes like pets.

It didn't take long for me to spot *him* in the line.

Julian.

He wore a blue tunic and breeches that matched his eyes. He stood next to a stunning faerie with shimmery pink wings and golden hair that fell to her waist. She smiled up at him, reaching up to push his dark blond hair off his forehead.

The gesture was so intimate. And from the way she was gazing up at him, it was clear to anyone who wasn't blind that there was something going on between them.

Betrayal twisted in my heart, so intensely that it physically hurt.

Right then, Julian turned his head, his ice blue eyes meeting mine. We stood there, frozen like that for what felt like ages, but in reality, was only a few seconds. All I could focus on was him.

"It hurts to want what you can't have," Devyn said, bringing me out of my Julian-induced haze. "Doesn't it?"

The pink-winged faerie intertwined her hand with Julian's, and I looked away, not wanting to see the two of them together.

Anger crackled through me again. Not only had Julian played me for a fool back in LA, but he'd been involved with a beautiful faerie princess the entire time. I felt like an even bigger idiot than before.

"I'm surprised that faeries are permitted to date half-bloods," I said instead, not wanting to acknowledge his statement about wanting what I couldn't have.

"Princess Ciera does appear to be enamored with Julian." Devyn watched the two of them, amused. "We have no rules against such things here. If the two of them want to have their fun together, no one's stopping them. But it would get no farther than fun. A faerie cannot become betrothed to a half-blood. Which, I suspect, is why Princess Ciera is nominating Julian for the Faerie Games."

"What do you mean?" I asked.

"If Julian is chosen to play in the Games, and if he wins, he'll become immortal and will be granted the privileges of a full-blood fae," he said. "Including the permission to wed any fae he'd like. With her consent, of course. Which it seems Princess Ciera will be more than happy to give."

So that was why Julian was here. For love.

For a reason I couldn't explain, knowing that made me feel sicker than before.

"If she really loved him, she wouldn't risk his life like that," I muttered, stealing another glance at them and quickly turning away.

"People do crazy things to be with the ones they love," he said.

Before I could ask him if he was referring to anything in particular, a burst of light exploded from the sky with a loud boom. For a second, it was like there were two suns. But then one of the suns got closer, and I realized it wasn't a sun at all.

It was a man on a golden chariot led by eight winged horses. He was bigger than any man I'd seen before. He must have been ten feet tall. An inhuman glow—like an aura—surrounded him, the chariot, and the horses.

He wasn't a man at all.

He was a god.

As he got closer, everyone started clapping and cheering. I simply gawked at the glowing god above us. It was impossible not to.

He circled a few times overhead, his sparkling light shining down upon us and trailing in his wake. He held a staff with a giant pinecone on top. Tiny golden orbs— each one about the size of a fist—flew out of the pinecone and followed in his wake, dispersing around the area. They situated themselves in various places, surrounding us on all angles.

Devyn moved closer to me. "They're projection orbs," he said, only for me to hear. "Similar to the cameras on Earth. They record the Games so everyone in the citadel can watch and enjoy the competition as it plays out in real time."

One of the orbs hummed behind me. I turned around and glared at it. It inched closer, and I immediately turned away. I did *not* want that thing in my face.

The god did a few more circular loops, dispersing more orbs from the pinecone staff. Finally, he pulled on the reins of the winged horses and led them down to the ground.

The chariot landed right in front of the Stone of Destiny and he stepped off of it, letting his eyes linger on the still-cheering crowd. He was as confident as ever in his gold toga, a headpiece of vines and grapes interwoven in his long dark hair. And there was a mischievous glint in his eyes, like he was ready for a party.

Staff in one hand, he raised his other hand in the air, and everyone went quiet. "I am Bacchus, god of wine and celebration," he announced, his voice booming through the hills. He snapped his fingers, and a huge goblet of wine suitable for someone his size appeared in his hand. He raised it in a toast with so much force that some of the wine splashed on the ground by his feet. "And as always, I'll be your host for the annual Faerie Games!"

His enthusiasm was infectious, and the crowd erupted into claps and cheers again. As they cheered, he raised the goblet to his lips and chugged the wine in seconds. He upended the goblet—proving he'd finished it all—and the cheering grew louder.

I'd never been to a fraternity party before, but this was what I imagined one might be like.

The goblet disappeared with another snap of his fingers. He slammed his staff down onto the ground, and everyone grew silent once again. He let his eyes roam along the line of us, studying us.

Prince Devyn and I were last, thanks to our late arrival. If we'd been any later, we would have missed the start of the ceremony.

I had a sneaking suspicion that was on purpose. Which was annoying, because I hated being last. When I needed to do something, I liked to get it done as quickly as possible. Otherwise I just stood around getting more and more anxious.

When Bacchus's eyes met mine, I stood strong, like most all the other half-bloods did before me. I didn't know much about the Faerie Games. But I knew that now was *not* the time to look weak.

Luckily, the god didn't look at me for long.

He quickly returned to face the center of the line. "A promising looking group of half-bloods," he said appreciatively. "The faerie princes and princesses have chosen well."

Many of them stood taller at the compliment, their colorful wings sparkling brighter as they beamed at the god.

"But only up to eleven of you will be chosen to play in the Games," he continued. "It all depends on who my fellow gods decide is worthy to receive the gift of their powers. So let's not stand around waiting any longer." Bacchus raised his staff again and sparklers shot out from the pinecone, exploding into fireworks in the sky. "It's time for the nomination ceremony to begin!"

21

SELENA

STARTING with the first in line, each faerie prince or princess led his or her nominated half-blood to the Stone of Destiny. The faerie announced the half-blood's name, and the half-blood stepped onto the tiles of rock surrounding the bottom of the Stone, facing the crowd.

Three half-bloods had approached the Stone so far.

Nothing interesting had happened.

"Maximus Murphy," Bacchus said the name of the red headed half-blood currently standing in front of the Stone of Destiny. "You have not been chosen by a god for this year's Faerie Games. Please step down and proceed to the viewing stand with your faerie patron."

Maximus stepped down and walked to the bleachers with the bristling faerie prince who had nominated him.

There, they joined the two other half-bloods who hadn't been chosen, along with their faerie patrons. Disappointment was clear on most of their faces, although I could have sworn that Maximus let out a small sigh of relief.

I didn't blame him. As far as I was concerned, not being chosen was a good thing.

I prayed that at the end of the ceremony I'd be standing on the bleachers with everyone else that hadn't been chosen.

Next, a beautiful faerie princess with gold wings that matched her hair led her half-blood to the Stone. She squared her shoulders and faced Bacchus. "I present my nominee, Felix Burns," she said proudly.

Felix stepped up to the Stone with the swagger of someone who always got what he wanted in life. When he turned to face us, it was clear why.

With his high cheekbones and strong jawline, he was James Dean's doppelganger. His naturally highlighted hair was tousled in a way that looked both casual and purposeful. He was almost *too* perfect looking. Although from the way every female on the hill gazed up at him—faeries and half-bloods alike—they clearly disagreed. A few of the men appeared enamored with him, too.

"Gods of Olympus," Bacchus said, his voice echoing

near and far. "Do any of you choose Felix Burns as your champion for this year's Faerie Games?"

After the last three anticlimactic nominations, I didn't expect anything to happen.

But this time, the stone hummed and glowed pink. The glow extended outward into a giant sphere, consuming Felix within it until he was no longer visible.

My breath caught in my chest, and I stood on my tiptoes to get a better view. The sphere swirled and sparkled, like a crystal ball. It continued doing that for about thirty seconds more. Then the Stone sucked the glow back inside of it, revealing Felix standing in the same place as before.

But now, Felix had wings. Bright, sparkly, pinks wings identical to those of the faeries. Behind him, the Stone glowed with the pink symbol of a heart.

The faerie princess who had nominated him clutched her hands to her chest and stared up at him with pride.

"Felix Burns," Bacchus said his name with newfound respect. "You have been chosen by Venus, the goddess of love! Congratulations on this great honor. Come take your place behind me, where we'll welcome the rest of the chosen champions for this year's Faerie Games."

Felix stepped down from the Stone, and the faerie princess who had nominated him pulled him into a tight embrace. She whispered something in his ear before heading over to the bleachers, where she took a spot in the previously empty front row.

Felix marched to stand behind Bacchus, an arrogant smirk on his face as he looked at the rest of us in line. He was so cocky that he already looked like he expected to win, and the rest of the players weren't even chosen yet.

I didn't like him already.

Nothing happened during the next few nominations. The half-bloods and their faerie patrons all joined the others who weren't chosen on the bleachers.

Each time I stepped forward in line, my stomach twisted with knots.

The next chosen half-blood was a girl with long black hair named Octavia. But instead of pink, the Stone glowed ocean blue for her. When the sphere around her disappeared, she had ocean blue wings. The symbol of a trident blazed blue in the Stone.

"Chosen by Neptune, the god of the sea!" Bacchus announced, and Octavia stepped down from the Stone to take her place behind the god.

She stood next to Felix, and as she checked him out, the two of them shared a knowing look. I could practically hear the unspoken challenge between them.

Game on.

A few more half-bloods were chosen by gods, although most were sent to the bleachers. We were about at the halfway point of the ceremony. And with every step I took closer to the Stone of Destiny, my body trembled more and more with nerves.

Finally, it was Julian's turn.

Princess Ciera led him up to the Stone. She stood on her tiptoes and gave him a light kiss on the cheek before turning to Bacchus. "I present my nominee," she said, meeting Bacchus's gaze straight on. "Julian Kane."

Julian took his spot in front of the Stone of Destiny. As he did, his eyes met mine and stayed there. It was like he was studying me, memorizing me.

I stilled, trapped in his ice-blue gaze. It was just like when I'd first seen him at the bottom of Torrence's driveway. I didn't think I could have looked away even if I'd wanted to.

"Gods of Olympus," Bacchus said, although his voice sounded muffled as I focused on Julian. "Do any of you choose Julian Kane as your champion for this year's Faerie Games?"

The Stone hummed, a steel gray glow forming around it and embracing Julian within its sphere. As with the others before him, the glowing orb sparkled and swirled as it worked its magic.

Once the magic was sucked back into the Stone,

Julian stood proudly, his new steel gray wings sparkling behind him. The symbol of two intercrossed swords shined from the Stone.

His eyes were still locked on mine, as mine were on his. Sure, Felix was the most traditionally handsome of everyone on the hill—faeries included. But something about Julian called to me. Like his soul was igniting mine. Like it was somehow *connected* to mine.

But I shook the thought away. The feelings I had were for the person I thought he was when we went on our date in LA. Not for who he really was—a conniving half-blood who'd kidnapped me to the Otherworld for money.

Julian was playing in the Games for Princess Ciera. So they could be together forever.

So why was he looking at me and not at her?

"Chosen by Mars, the god of war!" Bacchus's voice yanked me out of my thoughts.

Julian simply nodded, like he'd expected this. As he stepped down to join the other chosen champions, Princess Ciera pulled him close and gave him one final kiss on the cheek.

I averted my eyes, since seeing them together sent daggers through my heart. It was like every piece of my soul was screaming at me that Julian was *mine* and that Princess Ciera shouldn't be touching him.

Which was ridiculous and pathetic.

I needed to get over this stupid crush. Because logically, I hated him. He'd played me and used me. Whatever feelings I was having for him needed to *go away*.

If only I could force my heart to agree with my brain.

22

SELENA

THE CEREMONY CONTINUED, and more half-bloods were chosen by gods. Now, ten of them stood behind Bacchus, their wings sparkling behind them. No two half-bloods had the same color wings. Their wing colors all represented the god that had chosen them.

Bacchus got more and more excited each time a half-blood was chosen. Apparently, having ten half-bloods selected was extremely rare—and exciting for the faeries and gods.

The more half-bloods chosen, the more there were to watch being slaughtered.

"I don't know why we're bothering to continue," the girl in front of me said. They were the first words she'd spoken to me the entire time we'd been standing there, and she sounded annoyed and bitter. "None of us will be chosen."

"Bacchus said up to eleven of us could be chosen." I definitely remembered that detail. I'd been counting, hoping all eleven would be chosen before it was my turn at the Stone of Destiny.

"Technically, yes," she said. "But Jupiter's never chosen a champion in the history of the Games. No half-blood has ever been worthy to the king of the gods."

The faerie princess who was nominating her reached for her wrist and glared at her. "Shush," she said, her dark green eyes blazing with irritation. "You're already a disappointment for not being chosen. Don't make more of a spectacle of yourself now."

The girl pressed her lips together and turned around, not looking back at me again.

Did she actually want to be chosen? I wouldn't have believed it, except that all of the chosen half-bloods looked proud to be standing behind Bacchus.

They were either all confident that they'd win, or desperate to get out of whatever living situations they had to deal with. Given the dark circles under the eyes of most half-bloods on the bleachers, my bet was on the latter.

The ceremony continued, and everyone ahead of me

took their turns at the Stone of Destiny. None of them were chosen.

Prince Devyn and I were the only ones left. All eyes were on me, and I wanted to sink into the ground and disappear.

Devyn gave me a pointed look and walked toward Bacchus.

Like the half-bloods before me, I followed his lead, making sure to remain slightly behind him.

Relax, I told myself, trying to breathe steadily and calm down. *The Faerie Games have been happening for over fifteen hundred years. If Jupiter's never chosen a champion, that isn't going to change now.*

Still, I wouldn't feel better until I was standing on the bleachers with all the other rejects.

Devyn gave Bacchus a small smile. "I present my nominee," he said. "My daughter, Selena Pearce."

Chatter erupted from the bleachers, and I had a feeling why. None of the other faeries had announced any personal connection to their nominee.

Devyn had either gone off script, or no other faerie prince or princess would nominate their own flesh and blood. Or maybe they were simply shocked that Devyn *had* a daughter, since I hadn't set foot in the Otherworld since yesterday.

A golden orb buzzed around me, like it was trying to zoom in on my face. I fought every instinct to swat it away, although I couldn't help myself from giving it an annoyed, angry glare.

Bacchus pounded his staff against the ground so forcefully that the vibration rolled across the hill, sending everyone back into silence.

The god stared at me, waiting for me to approach the Stone of Destiny.

My body was cold to the bones, my feet heavy like lead. I didn't want to move. I wanted to tell Bacchus that I didn't want to be nominated.

But from the intense way the god was staring at me, I suspected he might smite me on the spot if I voiced my thoughts aloud.

I'd never get back home to Avalon if I got myself killed now.

Besides, all ten players had already been chosen. The smartest thing to do was lay as low as possible. Which meant doing what was expected of me and not making a spectacle of myself. Especially since not only everyone here, but apparently everyone in the entire citadel, was watching this ceremony play out live. The annoying floating orbs were enough of a reminder of that.

And so, I stepped up to the Stone, turning my back to

it and facing Bacchus like all the nominees had done before me.

"Gods of Olympus," Bacchus said, his devilish gaze locked on mine. "Do any of you choose Selena Pearce as your champion for this year's Faerie Games?"

23

SELENA

HUMMING BUZZED BEHIND ME, so intense that every inch of my skin prickled with awareness.

One moment, I was staring out at Bacchus, Prince Devyn, and the ten chosen champions before me.

The last thing I saw before an orb of light blue magic surrounded me was the shocked look on Bacchus's face.

There was nothing below me, nothing above me, and nothing around me. Just the light blue magic that seemed to stretch out into eternity. It sparkled and swirled, trapping me in what felt like another dimension.

Then, a man popped into existence in front of me. He was taller than Bacchus—he must have been twelve feet tall, at least. And he was ageless, with long white hair past his shoulders and a gold toga tied at his waist to show off his hard, chiseled chest. His eyes glowed an inhuman white, and I felt tiny under his intimidating gaze.

I couldn't move. All I could do was stare up at him in terrified awe.

"Selena Pearce." His voice boomed through the magical orb, making it shake like thunder. "I've been waiting over a millennia for a half-blood worthy of receiving the gift of my powers. Now, that time has come. I choose you to play for me in this year's Faerie Games."

A thick bolt of lightning flashed to life in his hand, and he shot it forward, straight at my heart.

I doubled over, screaming out in pain as the lightning crackled through my body like wildfire, zapping me to the core. Every part of me was ablaze. Like I was being burned from the inside out.

He was killing me. This must be what it felt like to die.

It might have lasted for less than a minute, or it could have been an eternity. But each torturous second was one too long to bear.

Finally, the blaze found release, exiting through my back between my shoulder blades. It was like a reservoir of power being emptied through a dam. And as the pain lessened, so did my screams.

Once I was able to open my eyes again, I saw flashes of light blue over my shoulders.

Wings. I'd grown wings. Sparkly, beautiful, light blue wings that shimmered with powerful magic.

And the god who'd stood before me moments before was nowhere to be found.

He'd disappeared as quickly as he'd arrived.

The magic surrounding me evaporated until I was back on the hill, staring at Bacchus, Devyn, and the chosen half-bloods. Every single one of them—including the crowd in the bleachers—gawked at me in shock, awe, and disbelief.

Well, every one of them except Devyn. He was as calm and confident as ever.

He'd known this was going to happen. Of course he had. That was the nature of his gift.

And he'd orchestrated the scene perfectly, down to making sure we were the last ones in line.

He was a manipulative, conniving, self-serving jerk.

Bacchus cleared his throat, apparently needing to get ahold of himself before speaking. "Congratulations, Selena Pearce," he finally said, surprise evident in his voice as it carried across the silenced crowd. "You just made history. Because you're the first half-blood ever chosen to play in the Faerie Games by the king of the gods himself—Jupiter."

24

SELENA

Everything was a blur as I took my spot in the line of chosen half-bloods behind Bacchus. My feet felt like they moved on their own, and while I heard chattering around me, I couldn't make out anything being said.

Because I was going to have to fight all these people beside me.

To the death.

I was going to die.

Bacchus had us all pose for a picture, which was taken by the golden orbs. The flash echoed in my vision after the photo was taken.

"Relax," a warm voice said from next to me, soothing me with its perfect cadence. Julian. "Jupiter chose you for a reason. You're strong enough to get through this. Just take it one step at a time."

I looked over at him and glared. I didn't know what irritated me more—that he was trying to calm me down, or that it was working.

Because he was right. I needed to take this one step at a time. I needed to focus on staying alive until my parents and their army came to the Otherworld to rescue me.

They were probably on their way here now. It wouldn't be long until I was back home, where I belonged.

But I felt my glare at Julian soften. It was like his caring blue eyes intoxicated my soul and turned my brain to mush.

I shook off the unwanted feelings. "I know I'm strong enough," I said, my tone laced with venom. "I don't need *you* to tell me that." I turned away from him, not wanting to be affected by him the way I was. Everyone in the Faerie Games was going to be pitted against each other. The other players were my enemies.

It would do me no good to be crushing on an enemy.

Before Julian could reply, Bacchus spoke again. "In four days, all eleven of you will enter Vesta's Villa, and the Faerie Games will begin," he said. "In the meantime, it's time to return to the homes of the faerie that nominated you to prepare for your grand entrance." He turned to face the orbs, smiling at them with glee. "I'm

Bacchus, god of celebration and master of the Faerie Games ceremonies," he said, clearly speaking to the viewers now and not to us. "Tune in Friday to watch the chosen champions give us a sneak peek of their new powers before they enter the villa. I can't wait to see what this year's contestants are made of."

The crowd in the bleachers clapped and hollered in agreement.

He snapped his fingers, another goblet of wine appearing in his hand, and raised it in a toast toward the orbs. "Cheers, and I'll see you soon!"

25

SELENA

THE ORBS STOPPED GLOWING, and the faeries that nominated us rushed to our sides, ushering us back to the carriages. Once in our carriage, Devyn explained that the chosen champions weren't supposed to speak to each other until we entered the villa. In the villa, the orbs would be recording us twenty-four seven—even while we were sleeping.

I shuddered at the thought. Having an entire country of faeries watching my every move for entertainment was downright creepy.

As he spoke, I stared at him, piecing things together in my mind. "You have omniscient sight," I said. "You said you cared about me. You wouldn't have nominated me unless you knew I was going to win."

"As I told you earlier, the future is never set in stone,"

he said. "Despite my gift, I can't truly know anything until it happens."

"But you know what futures are more likely to happen than others."

"I also know that anything I say about the future has the potential to change it." His violet eyes that matched my own were hard as he stared me down. "Don't question me, Selena. You won't like the outcome if you do."

The rest of the chariot ride was spent in silence, and not by my choice. I wanted to learn everything I could about the Faerie Games so I'd have the best chance of winning. But Devyn refused to answer my questions.

I supposed it was because he didn't want to change the current future.

Eventually I gave up asking him anything and sat back, watching the rolling green hills pass by as we made our way back to the city. According to Bacchus, I had four days before entering the villa.

So if Devyn refused to prepare me for the Games, I'd simply have to find someone who would.

It was nighttime when we got back, and two half-blood servants walked me to my room. My window now featured an image I'd recognize anywhere—the luscious, tropical mountains of Avalon.

The sight of my home felt like a stab in my heart.

Nessa was either trying to make me homesick, or she was trying to remind me what I was fighting for. But her intentions didn't matter. Because the sight of Avalon fired me up to get back there, no matter what I needed to do to make it happen.

Now that I was alone, I studied my shimmery, light blue wings in the mirror. Made of light, they sparkled with each movement I made. I couldn't help smiling as I looked at them. Because while the wings should have felt foreign, they didn't. It was like they'd always been a part of me, and they were relieved to finally be out in the open for the rest of the world to see.

It was like I was seeing my true self for the first time.

But whatever Jupiter had done to me must have drained me, because it wasn't long before my head felt heavy, the bed in my room calling me to it. I wanted to fight sleep, but what would be the point? Tomorrow was going to come, whether I wanted it to or not. I might as well face it awake instead of exhausted.

So I changed into pajamas, expecting the wings to be a hindrance in getting dressed. But my clothes passed through them, as if the wings were made of nothing at all. It was extraordinary. Especially because when I touched the wings, I felt their warm, crackling energy under my fingertips. They were tangible, yet not at the same time. Incredible.

Hopefully they wouldn't be uncomfortable while I slept.

But I didn't find out one way or another, because the moment my head hit the pillow, I sank into a deep, dreamless sleep.

26

SELENA

Two men—one with bright pink wings and the other with deep green wings—burst into my room, startling me awake.

The man with pink wings wore a pink sequined tunic with matching breeches. The green winged man was tall, dark skinned, and had a clean-shaven head. He wore loose fitting, black breeches and no top, presumably to show off his chiseled chest.

"Good morning, Princess!" the man with pink wings said in an overly peppy voice that *no one* should be allowed to use so early in the morning. "Rise and shine! We have work to do, and not much time to do it."

The green-winged man looked me over and crossed his arms, which were just as built and toned as his chest.

"Nessa told us you needed our help," he said. "And damn, was she right. You're a mess. A hot one, but still a mess."

"But no worries!" the pink-winged man jumped in, his light purple eyes wide with glee. "Bryan and Finn are here to come to your rescue!" He twirled and struck a pose, glitter fluttering out of his wings as he spun. Some of it landed in his hair—I suspected on purpose.

"What's going on?" I sat up, rubbing sleep out of my eyes as I looked back and forth between the two of them. "Who are you?"

"I'm Bryan," the pink-winged man said, and then he pointed his thumb to the shirtless, green-winged man next to him. "And this gorgeous, perfect specimen of man is Finn. Prince Devyn chose us to prep you for the Faerie Games."

"Prep me how?" I asked, feeling instantly more awake at the prospect of being prepared for the Games.

"I'm your stylist." Bryan motioned to himself and struck another pose. "Now that you're chosen for the Games, you're no longer relegated to the bland, boring styles of half-bloods. You'll need someone to dress and style you like a fae. Which is where my expertise comes into play."

"Oh." I deflated, knowing my reaction was far from the excitement he wanted.

"What's wrong, honey?" His eyes flashed with concern.

"I thought you were here to teach me how to win the Games," I said. "Not to dress me up like some kind of faerie princess."

"Presenting yourself well *will* help you win the Games," he said. "The gods claim the competitions are fair, but trust me, they're not. They're catered to the strengths of the players the faeries want to see win. And faeries respect good style. It's why half-bloods have the awful dress code rules they do." He grimaced at the thought, although he returned to his perky self a moment later. "They're not allowed to outshine the fae. I'll also be teaching you social strategies for the Games, which can be more important than the physical part."

"But don't worry," Finn said, his voice booming through the room. "I'm here to teach you how to use your new powers."

Electricity crackled through me at his words, and when I looked down at my hands, they were *glowing*. Bright streaks of white lightning moved through my palms, traveling up toward my elbows.

For the first time in my life, I didn't just *feel* my power.

I *saw* it.

"You have the same power I do?" I asked Finn.

"No," he said. "Jupiter's never chosen a contestant for the Games. So no one's ever trained a half-blood gifted with his powers. But Prince Devyn has his reasons for everything, including reasons for choosing us for this job. I'm one of the best trainers in the Otherworld. If anyone can prepare you for the Games, it's me."

"He's being modest." Bryan placed a loving hand on Finn's bicep. "Finn is *the* best trainer in the Otherworld." He turned to face me again, excitement in his eyes as he bounced on the tips of his toes. "Now, get your gorgeous, blond head out of bed! Because it's time to start your training."

27

SELENA

FINN LEFT to prepare the courtyard for my training, and Bryan stayed to get me ready. He dressed me in a shimmery, flared blue mini-dress with matching thigh-high boots. Even my eyes had light blue sparkly eye shadow on them.

Since light blue was my wing color, I was supposed to stick to the color scheme with my clothing throughout the Games.

"You can't be serious," I said, studying my reflection in the mirror.

"Why not?" He frowned in disappointment at my reaction. "You look stunning."

"I look like I'm ready for a Halloween party. Not for magic training."

"Halloween?" His forehead knitted in confusion, but

then he appeared to put it together. "Oh, right. That's what they call Samhain on Earth now." I opened my mouth to protest again, but he continued talking before I had a chance. "I can assure you, this dress would *never* do for the Samhain ball," he said. "You'd need something far more fabulous for that. Now, come on. Finn is waiting in the courtyard, and while I love the man, patience has never been a virtue of his." He strutted out of the room, pink sparkles trailing in his wake.

I simply sighed again as I looked at the ridiculous outfit in the mirror and followed his lead. Because at the end of the day, what I was wearing was the least of my concerns.

What mattered most was learning how to use my new powers.

When I arrived in the courtyard, I found that Finn had placed various objects of different sizes on pedestals throughout the space. The objects were truly random—everything from a single grape to a stone the size of a basketball that looked suspiciously like a diamond.

"Let's start easy," Finn said, walking to stand behind the pedestal with the single green grape. "I want you to touch this grape and incinerate it."

As I walked toward the grape, I thought about the invitation Iris had given me for my birthday party, and how I'd unsuccessfully tried to incinerate it. That night felt worlds away right now. But the urge to incinerate things had always been a part of me. I'd just never been able to harness it.

Lightning crackled through me at the possibility that being chosen by Jupiter might have changed things. And while I hated the circumstances that had brought me to the Otherworld, and the ones that had made me a player in the Faerie Games, I also felt empowered by the knowledge that I might have the power I'd craved for my entire life. I'd no longer be a pawn on someone else's chessboard.

Finally, I might be able to control my own destiny.

The thought made the lightning crackle all the way down to my toes. My body glowed with bolts of magic, and I couldn't wait to release it.

I reached for the grape, ready to let loose on it. My fingers touched its soft surface and all the lightning building inside of me rushed outward in a blinding flash, an explosive crack filling the courtyard.

The flash only lasted for a second. When it ended, it wasn't only the grape that was gone.

The entire pedestal was gone, too.

The pedestal had been made of stone. Now all that remained of it was a pile of ashes on the ground.

I flexed my fist, excitement buzzing through me at the realization that I'd been responsible for that.

"I asked you to incinerate the grape." Finn looked at the ashes and then back to me, smirking. "Not the entire pedestal."

"Sorry." I shrugged, unable to help smiling back. "I let out the lightning, and it just kind of... happened."

"It's certainly impressive for a first try," he said. "But you'll need to *control* your magic if you want to win the Faerie Games. So we have some serious work to do."

———

By mid-day, I'd incinerated over half of the courtyard with my electric touch. No matter what I tried, I couldn't control the force of my lightning.

As we continued, I grew hungry and tired. And as I tired, the power of my lightning weakened, too. Until finally, I managed to incinerate only a single grape, and not the entire pedestal it sat upon.

We broke for lunch, and I was so famished that I ate more than twice as much as Finn and Bryan. We didn't have any water, of course—fae clearly thought water was beneath them. But we didn't have wine, either. We had a honey flavored, non-alcoholic fruit juice called nectar that tasted similar to the wine I'd shared with Devyn. After all, I still had training to do, and I couldn't be tipsy while doing it.

The nectar must have refueled me, because by the time we finished lunch, I was ready to continue training.

Now that I was back at full strength, my lightning was back to being out of control. I tried to rein it in, but the electric jolts I sent out with my hands had a life of their own.

"This won't do," Finn said after I'd destroyed nearly every piece of furniture in the courtyard. It looked like multiple bombs had gone off. The only object that survived the force of my magic was the massive diamond ball. "If this is what happens when you *touch* things, I don't want to think about what will happen once you let out bolts at full blast."

"Isn't this a good thing?" I wiped at the soot on my cheeks. "Don't I want to be able to protect myself?"

"You can't protect yourself if you can't control yourself," he said. "There will be times during the Games when you'll be asked to maim—not to kill. If you accidentally kill during those competitions, you'll be expelled from the Games." His eyes darkened with warning when he said the final part. "And only one chosen champion—the winner—is allowed to walk out of the Games alive."

"So by 'expelled,' you mean 'killed,'" I guessed.

"Yes." He nodded. "The overseer of the Games—Juno —decides on the punishments for rule breaking. She's Jupiter's queen. And who knows how Juno will react to the fact that her husband gifted his powers to a beautiful blond half-blood. She's the jealous type. Especially toward young women who catch her husband's eye."

"It wasn't like that with Jupiter." The intimidating god who'd bestowed these powers upon me had looked at me like a pawn in his game—nothing more. "He barely even spoke to me."

"It won't matter," Bryan piped in. "Juno will assume you seduced her husband and are carrying on an illicit affair with him. She'll be eager to get rid of you."

"But she's a god." Frustration coursed through my veins, giving more power to the lightning raging inside of me. "Doesn't she see everything? Shouldn't she know the truth?"

"The gods are more powerful than any other beings in the universe, but they're just as infallible as anyone else," Bryan said. "They're not omniscient."

"No," I said. "That's just my father."

Venom laced my tone as I spoke of him, and silence descended amongst the three of us.

"You'll learn how to control your magic," Finn said, changing the subject away from Prince Devyn. "Because if you accidentally show the other players the full force of your magic, they're going to see you as a threat. It'll make you an early target—more than you already are, since you're the first player ever chosen by Jupiter."

"So not only does Juno hate me, but the other players will be gunning for me off the bat, too," I muttered. "Great."

My chance of survival was looking worse by the minute.

"It's not as awful as it sounds," Finn said, although if he was trying to be reassuring, it wasn't working. "I'm the best trainer in the Otherworld for a reason. But perhaps it's best to give your magic a rest for a bit. In the meantime, how good are you at using a sword?"

"I can hold my own." I smiled, thinking about the combat classes I'd taken on Avalon. I wasn't the best in the class, but I was far from the worst.

"Glad to hear it." Finn looked to Bryan, who flitted out of the courtyard, returning quickly with two bronze swords.

Bryan handed one to Finn, and the other to me. It felt strange in my hand—lighter than the steel swords we used on Avalon. But that made sense, since the fae were allergic to iron. Steel swords had no use to them.

Finn held his sword at the ready, circling me in challenge. He was playful, yet menacing as the warrior within him broke through the surface. "Come on, Princess," he said, flashing me a predatory smile. "It's time to show me what you've got."

28

SELENA

THE GOOD NEWS was that according to Finn, I was talented enough with weapons to possibly stay alive for a decent portion of the Faerie Games.

The bad news was that after the second day of training, I still couldn't control my lightning enough to stop the courtyard from looking like a war zone.

"Let's try something different," Finn said, looking around at the destruction surrounding us. "We know you can harness lightning in your body and incinerate objects with a touch. But I've yet to see you produce any visible bolts to strike from afar."

I raised an eyebrow. "Didn't you say that would be even more destructive than what I'm doing now?"

"This courtyard is magically enforced," he said, which I already knew, since it was all as good as new when we'd come back to train this morning. "And we're not getting anywhere by doing the same thing over and over. So let's try switching it up."

"This is going to be good." Bryan shimmied from where he was relaxing on a lounge chair in the sun, sipping a glass of honeyed wine.

"All right." I turned back to Finn, determined to do a good job at whatever challenge was next. "What do you want me to do?"

"See the big diamond?" He glanced at the basketball sized diamond gleaming on top of one of the few remaining pedestals.

I nodded, since it was impossible to miss.

"I want you to gather as much lightning as possible and shoot it toward the diamond to incinerate it. From right where you're standing now."

I eyed the diamond, which was about fifteen feet away. It had withstood my jolts when I'd touched it. But if Finn was right and an actual bolt was more powerful than my touch, I should be able to blow it to smithereens if I put enough power behind my magic.

"Okay." I stood steady on my feet, staring down at the diamond as I gathered the buzzing, crackling magic within me. "Here goes nothing."

I held my hands up and aimed my lightning straight at the diamond.

Nothing happened.

The magic crackled on my palms, lighting them up with magic, but that was it. No matter how hard I tried pushing my magic outward, the bolt I was imagining in my mind refused to form.

"Hm." Finn crossed his arms, pressing his lips together. "Interesting."

"Why?" I lowered my arms back down to my sides, the lightning within them fizzling out. "Was that supposed to happen?"

"I have no idea what was supposed to happen," he said. "You're the first half-blood ever gifted with Jupiter's powers. Your training is a learning process for all of us."

"Great." I brushed my palms off on my stupidly gaudy dress as if I could wipe away my failure. "That's just great."

"That wasn't what I expected to happen, but that's why we're doing these tests," he said. "So we can learn what to expect *before* the Games begin. If you can't create lightning bolts, we need to train you to control your electric touch. Bryan, go fetch the rats."

"Rats?" I backed away in disgust. "For what?"

"It's time to see what happens when you use your magic on living creatures."

"No." I shook my head and crossed my arms over my

chest. "No way. You saw what I did to a freaking grape. I'm *not* testing my magic on innocent animals."

The two faeries looked at each other in concern.

"I understand your hesitation," Finn said, kinder than ever before. "Trust me, I don't like this any more than you do. I know you don't know much about our kind, but fae love and appreciate all nature—animals included. But sometimes we have to do hard things for the greater good. We've yet to discover what your magic will do to a living creature. And while no creature should suffer without reason, there *is* a reason why we're doing this. Because it's better to accidentally kill a rat while you're training than to accidentally kill one of your fellow players when you're not supposed to."

There was so much wrong with what he'd just said that I could barely process what shocked me most.

No, that was a lie.

Because what shocked me most was that I'd eventually be expected to kill the other players in the Faerie Games. If I didn't, they'd kill me first.

And if I accidentally killed one of them in a competition that wasn't to the death... well, Finn had already told me what would happen to me then. Juno would punish me by killing me.

That certainly wasn't an option.

"What's on your mind, Princess?" Bryan asked,

placing his wine glass down on the little table next to his lounge chair.

I turned to him, unable to hide the defeat I felt throughout my body. "I don't want to kill anyone." My voice wavered with tears that threatened to come out at any second. But I swallowed them down, because if I started crying now, I wasn't sure I'd be able to stop. "I just want to go home."

He said nothing. Instead, he stood up, walked over to me, and wrapped me in a hug. And call me crazy, but it was like he was sending emotionally soothing magic from his body into mine. Not in a weird way, but in a familiar way. Like he was letting me know he was there for me when my parents couldn't be.

I needed that hug more than I cared to admit.

"I know this is a lot." Bryan pulled away and looked at me more seriously than ever. "But Finn and I are on your side. We're going to do everything we can to help you get through this alive, so you can get back home to Avalon. And if you play the Faerie Games strategically, you can get to the end with killing as minimally as possible."

"Really?" I said. "How?"

"Every week, there's a competition to determine the Emperor—or Empress—of the Villa," Finn said. "This competition isn't to the death. The Emperor of the Villa then chooses the three players he or she wants to battle in the Coliseum at the end of the week. Those three players fight in the arena until the first one is dead."

"So I need to make sure not to be chosen for those fights," I said.

"Exactly." Bryan nodded, smiling at me. "You catch on quick."

I smiled back at him, since it was true—I'd always been a fast learner. And the longer I could avoid being chosen to battle in the arena, the more time my family would have to come to the Otherworld and bring me home.

"You'll need to make strong alliances with the other players, so they won't choose you for the arena battles if they're Emperor of the Villa," Bryan said. "To make strong alliances, you need to prove you're a solid asset to the team... while not being *so* powerful that your alliance members get scared and want to get rid of you. It's a delicate balance, and you won't be able to manage it if you don't improve your control over your power. That's why Finn and I are training you now. To teach you everything we can to help you stay alive. But you need to work with us and trust that we have your best interests at heart. Can you do that?"

I looked between both of them, thinking about what he'd asked of me. I technically had no reason to trust any of the fae, since I was a prisoner in their world. But after the time I'd spent with Finn and Bryan, my gut instinct told me to trust them.

And while Prince Devyn was cold and distant, he was still my biological father. I didn't think he wanted me dead. He wouldn't have chosen Bryan and Finn as my trainers if they weren't the best choices to help keep me alive.

But I needed to help myself, too. Which meant doing as Bryan and Finn asked… even if they were asking me to do something hard.

"Yes," I finally said, standing stronger as I met both of their eyes. "I can do that."

"Great." Finn sighed with relief. "Bryan, go get those rats. We have training to do."

29

SELENA

TESTING my magic on rats was the incentive I needed to get my electric touch under control.

By the end of the next day, I could control the level of my "voltage," as Bryan had decided to call it. I could use it to shock and disable, without killing.

Which was good, because I didn't want any innocent rats—or people—dying under my watch.

"Excellent job." Bryan clapped from his lounge chair. "Now, I think you're ready to start testing on something bigger." He removed his sequined shirt, folded it neatly, and placed it on the chair. "This is one of my favorite shirts," he said, running his hands over it to flatten it out. "I won't risk it being singed."

"No." Finn crossed his arms and stared Bryan down.

"She's not testing her magic on you. I'm her trainer. She's testing it on me."

"But I'm the nicer of the two of us." Bryan looked over his shoulder and shot Finn a megawatt grin. "And by this point in training, she probably wants to hurt me less than she wants to hurt you."

"I'm not testing my magic on either of you," I said before they could continue this conversation further. "What if I accidentally kill you?"

"You won't," Bryan said. "You showed excellent control with the rats. And we full fae are made of strong stuff. We're harder to kill than that diamond over there. So since you still can't destroy the diamond, you definitely won't destroy us." He pranced toward me, ready to go. He was leaner than Finn, but still muscled.

His physique wasn't the first thing I noticed, though.

The first thing I noticed was the heart-shaped birthmark on the left side of his stomach.

Not because it was unique, which it was. But because Finn had an identical one on the same place on his stomach.

"The two of you have identical birthmarks." I looked between them to make sure I was correct. I was. "How's that possible?"

"These are more than just birthmarks." Bryan

reached forward and lovingly touched the mark on Finn's stomach. "They're soulmate marks."

"Most fae are marked on the day we're born," Finn said. "That mark matches the one on our soulmate. It helps us find each other."

"Not like we needed help finding each other," Bryan chimed in. "From the moment I saw Finn, I knew he was the one."

From the adoring way he looked at his soulmate—and from the similar way Finn looked at him—I didn't doubt it.

My fingers went to the clover shaped birthmark on my right hipbone. As they did, my thoughts went to Julian, and the stunned way he'd looked at me the moment we'd first seen each other. Like he'd been waiting to meet me for all his life.

But I needed to stop thinking about him. He'd only kissed me to get me close enough to the fountain so he could drag me through the portal. He'd brought me to the Otherworld in exchange for one bag of money.

I didn't like him, let alone want to be soulmates with him.

At least, I didn't *want* to want to be soulmates with him.

If only he weren't so gorgeous, and if only that kiss

hadn't felt so perfect. That would make it a lot easier to control my unwelcome feelings toward him.

"Do only full fae have soulmate marks?" I asked, unable to contain my curiosity. "Or can half-bloods have them, too?"

"It's mainly only full fae," Finn said. "A handful of half-bloods have had soulmates, but it's rare. There hasn't been a half-blood soulmate couple for over ninety years. And since half-bloods have similar lifespans to humans, they've already passed on to the Underworld."

"Oh." I deflated, sad even though I should have been relieved. "Okay."

"Why?" Bryan raised his eyebrows and rubbed his hands together, ready for gossip. "Is there someone special waiting for you back on Avalon?"

"Definitely not." I laughed, since I'd never had a boyfriend in my life. "There aren't any faeries on Avalon, or any half-bloods, either. Well, at least not other than me."

"Hm." Bryan lowered his hands, although he didn't look convinced. "Then perhaps there's someone special you've met since coming to the Otherworld?"

I looked away from him, not wanting him to see the truth of his words reflected in my eyes. He was far too intuitive. And while that normally wasn't a bad thing, right now I didn't like it at all.

"So, how about that training?" I said, desperate to change the subject before he could pry any farther. "If faeries are as indestructible as you say, it's time we found out exactly what my powers can do. Don't you think?"

"Now we're talking." Finn grinned. "But Bryan—and these are words I never thought I'd say—put your shirt back on. Because Selena's not going to test her magic on you. She's going to test it on me."

30

SELENA

THE NEXT MORNING, Bryan woke me before dawn to get me ready for the parade.

All chosen champions paraded down the street before entering Vesta's Villa. Once we entered the Villa, the Games would officially begin.

I pushed myself up from my bed, groggy after three days of such intense training. "Where's Finn?" I asked, since I'd expected both my trainers to be there.

"He's exhausted after all those electric shocks you gave him yesterday," Bryan said with a thin smile—a mix between pride about how I'd gained an acceptable level of control over my powers, and worry for his soulmate. "He'll see you out once you're ready. But this is your grand entrance, so getting you ready will be no short process. I figured it best not to wake him until it's time to see you off."

───────────

I gazed in the mirror, barely recognizing my reflection.

I wore an intricate light blue gown, with gold streaks running down the bottom half. The material shimmered, as if woven by magic. The top half was a mixture of light blue, gold, and cut-out sections that revealed far more of my skin than I was used to.

It was more scandalous than anything anyone wore on Avalon, and it seemed out of place for first thing in the morning. But Bryan assured me that he knew what he was doing. I trusted him, so I let him continue to do his thing.

He'd wound my hair up in strips of cloth last night, and when he removed the cloth, my hair tumbled down my back in perfect curls. Since I was chosen by a god to play in the Faerie Games, I now had higher status than a half-blood and was allowed to wear my hair accordingly. Bryan had instructed me *only* to wear my hair up during combat. I was to keep it down at all other times, to show my newly acquired place in Otherworld society.

He completed the outfit with a delicate golden headpiece that dropped down along my forehead, golden arm cuffs of swirling vines, and golden ear cuffs that gave my ears the illusion of being pointed at the edges like a full fae. The ear cuffs symbolized that even though I wasn't born a full fae, I now had the rank and privileges of one.

The entire outfit, combined with my sparkling wings, made me look strong, confident, and powerful.

I looked *ready* for the Faerie Games.

If only I felt as ready as I looked.

"Perfect," Bryan said, stepping backward to admire his handiwork. "Now, remember, I'll be watching your every move from the orb broadcasts and sending you outfits appropriate for whatever situation you find yourself in. All outfits will be approved by the council and delivered straight to your wardrobe."

He'd already explained why the outfits had to be approved by the council—so they could make sure he wasn't sending any notes in the pockets that would give me an advantage in the Games. Because once the other chosen players and I stepped into Vesta's Villa, we'd be cut off from the outside world. Every move we made in the Games was to be our own and not influenced by anyone on the outside.

"Yes." I nodded, feeling like I was looking at someone

else getting ready instead of myself. I felt strangely numb inside. Like the fact that I was being sent to compete in a twisted game to the death still hadn't set in. "I know."

He put shimmery gold eye shadow on my lids in the simple style he'd taught me how to do myself. I was far from an expert with applying makeup, but it didn't matter much in the Otherworld. Makeup here was only for decoration and self-expression. The magic in our wings enhanced our features in the way humans strived for with makeup and cosmetic surgery on Earth. The fae looked eerily perfect at all times. It was like seeing someone through a filtered phone lens.

"Selena Pearce, chosen champion of Jupiter," Bryan addressed me by my official title. His eyes were soft, and he looked down at me with a mix of pride and worry. "You're beautiful, both inside and out. I'm honored to have had the opportunity to help your natural beauty shine."

"Don't talk like that," I said.

"Like what?"

"Like you're sending me to my death."

He stood straighter and took my hands in his. "You're Prince Devyn's daughter, and you've been gifted magic from Jupiter—magic I believe you've only just begun tapping into," he said, each word searing itself into my soul. "Jupiter chose you for a reason. Something tells me that big things are coming in your future. And to get to that future, you're going to win the Games. So let's get you out there so you can show them what you're made of."

31

SELENA

I RODE in the flying carriage with Bryan, Finn, Nessa, and Prince Devyn toward the northeast of the country, where Vesta's Villa was located. The carriage magically expanded to make room for the five of us. But we rode there in total silence.

Devyn refused to talk to me, apparently because he didn't want to change my current future. And with him silent, the others followed suit. Even Bryan—who was normally as chatty as ever—didn't say a word.

So I stared out the window and ran through the lessons Bryan and Finn had taught me. There were three main things I needed to do to survive the Faerie Games:

Outwit.

Outfight.

Outlive.

I needed to play a good social game. I needed to fight and defend myself if—and *only* if—it was necessary. Most importantly, I needed to live.

I could do this. I *had* to do this. At least, I needed to stay alive until my parents found me and took me home.

Before I knew it, the winged horses started our descent, approaching a grassy hill in the middle of nowhere. It looked similar to the hill with the Stone of Destiny, but there was no stone in sight on this hill.

Here, there were eleven golden chariots, each with a magnificent horse at its head. And apparently Prince Devyn liked to make an entrance, because only one chariot was still empty. Mine.

A chosen half-blood stood on each chariot. Of course, my eyes first went to Julian, who stood strong with his sharp, steel colored wings behind him. My heart tightened, as if it were being physically pulled toward him.

Julian turned around to look straight at my carriage at that exact moment, and I couldn't help wondering if he felt the same pull toward me as I did to him. His eyes found mine through the window, and I stopped breathing, trapped in his gaze. He looked just as mesmerized by the sight of me as he had that night back in LA. I was sure I was looking back at him the same way.

But then he turned back around, and I wondered if the moment had really happened at all.

My hand automatically went to my right hip, where my birthmark was covered by my dress. I moved it away the moment I realized what I was doing.

Bryan cleared his throat, and my cheeks heated as I looked to him. "Remember one of the most important rules of the Game, Princess," he said, sounding way more cunning now that we were out in the field. "Don't fall in love with any of the other players, no matter how alluring they might be. Couples make the strongest alliances, and because of that, the other players fear them. They always get targeted early on. And even if they make it far, it can never end well, since only one player can win."

It wasn't an actual rule of the Games. But it was one of the rules Bryan had given me to help me win.

"I know," I said, although as I looked at Julian again, my heart hurt with the knowledge that if I was going to win, he and all the other chosen champions would have to die.

But I shook the thought away. Because my parents would get here and save me—and maybe the other players, too—before that could happen. They *had* to.

The Faerie Games were sick and twisted, and they went against everything Avalon believed in. Once my parents learned about what was going on here, they'd have the Nephilim army put an end to it once and for all.

The Nephilim army could be in the Otherworld right now, preparing to attack.

But they weren't here yet. And so, I got out of the carriage to head toward the empty chariot waiting for me.

Prince Devyn took my arm in his and led me there. "Good luck, Selena," he said, quietly enough so only I could hear. "And remember—no matter what you're faced with, always trust yourself and your instincts. They'll rarely steer you wrong."

It was the most he'd said to me in the past three days. It wasn't the first time he'd said it, either. So as I took my spot on the chariot, I replayed his words in my mind.

Trust myself and my instincts.

Devyn had said those exact words for a reason. Whatever that reason was, it was sure to be important. Perhaps he was even saying that trusting my instincts was the key to winning the Games.

He was gone before I had a chance to ask, rejoining Nessa, Bryan, and Finn at the carriage. When I looked back at them, Finn gave me a single nod. Almost as if he were saying, "You've got this."

Suddenly, the sky exploded with a loud boom. All

eyes immediately went up, where in a burst of light, Bacchus appeared in his horse-drawn chariot like he had before the Nomination Ceremony.

The glowing orbs dispersed out of his scepter, scattering around the area. One of them zoomed toward me, until it was buzzing about two feet away from my face. All the other chosen champions had an orb buzzing around them, too.

Bacchus settled down to the ground facing the row of us, although he didn't get off his chariot. "Good morning, Champions!" He grinned for the orb closest to him and let his eyes roam along the lineup of all of us. "You all look incredible. I love seeing the transformations after half-bloods get chosen for the Games. It shows what a true privilege it is to be chosen by the gods!" He grinned again, and the trainers and royal faeries that were representing us clapped from where they stood next to their carriages.

I glared at Bacchus, sure my expression was stone cold. Because even though Jupiter had given me magic, playing in the Faerie Games wasn't a *privilege*. Not when it resulted in all but one of us ending up dead.

But none of the other players looked as distressed as I felt. There was something else in their eyes.

Determination. Resolve. Ambition.

All eleven of us intended to win.

"I'm sure you're excited to step foot in Vesta's Villa," Bacchus continued once the clapping died down. "But first, we must show you off to the fae that journeyed here today from all across the citadel to see you in person. They're waiting along the road that leads to Vesta's Villa. So follow me, and let's give them a parade to remember!"

32

SELENA

THE FIRST PERSON in the line—Octavia, who'd been chosen by Neptune—gripped the reins of her horse and followed Bacchus. She stood strong and proud, her long dark hair flying behind her as she set off.

After her, each player followed in order down the line. I was at the end, which made me last.

A purposeful move of Prince Devyn's.

I held tightly onto the reins as Bacchus led us around a curve. Once we came around it, the road straightened, the sides of it packed with faeries. Their colorful clothes were woven with gold and studded with jewels, their wings shimmering in the sunlight.

They broke out into cheers of approval when they saw us.

The orbs flew over the crowd to get a better view of

the scene. The sides of the road were roped off, but the fae in the front reached forward as we passed, as if we were royalty. There were even kids in the audience, clinging onto their parents' hands and staring up at us in admiration.

They were all so happy, so excited. But didn't they realize they were sending all but one of us to a death sentence? Didn't they care?

No, I thought, recalling what Bryan had told me when I'd asked him the exact same thing during training. The fae believed that because we'd been chosen by the gods, there was a special place in the Underworld reserved just for us. Many even believed that once we died and crossed into the Underworld, we'd become gods ourselves.

In their minds, they weren't sending us to our deaths. They were sending us to a wonderful future.

The names of all the chosen champions who had crossed over to the Underworld were engraved on golden leaves inside the holiest temple in the capital city, so those of us who had fallen could be worshipped alongside the gods for the rest of time. That was why they called us all champions, even though only one of us could win the Games each year.

Because to the fae, we were all winners.

It was ludicrous. I believed in the Beyond—or the

Underworld, as they called it—as much as all supernaturals. But I had zero intention of going there before it was my time.

No way was my time going to happen now, when I was only sixteen years old. And my death sure as hell wasn't going to happen for the sake of entertaining the faeries and the gods.

I wanted to return home to Avalon and use my new magic for good.

If that meant doing what I needed to do to win the Faerie Games, then so be it. And that was only *if* the Nephilim army didn't find and save me first.

I must have been lost in thought, because before I knew it, we crested over a hill and Vesta's Villa came into view.

With everyone calling it a "villa," I'd been under the impression that the house would be modest in size.

How wrong I was.

Because it was a palace. An imposing, stone palace with vines and flowers wrapped around it that made it look almost like a part of nature. The main building in the center was three stories tall. Symmetrical wings jutted out of both sides, each decorated with columns and statues of the Roman gods.

The crowd parted at the gates, and Bacchus led the way to the bottom of a grand staircase that led up to the double door entrance of the villa. He stopped and turned around, watching as our horses led our chariots in a semicircle facing out toward the crowd. There was a fountain in the center of the drive, right in front of where Bacchus stood. Although the god was so tall that it didn't affect his view of the crowd.

Bacchus raised his scepter and shot two bursts of gold magic up into the sky—one to the right, and one to the left. They were giant orbs, and they showed a magnified version of Bacchus standing in front of the villa. Then the images panned around, showing each of us on our chariots facing the crowd.

The orbs were giant magical screens, so the fae in the back would be able to see what was happening. Small orbs still floated around us, and I assumed they were recording us and magically transmitting the recordings to be shown on the larger orbs. They were transmitting to everyone in the Otherworld, too.

Chills ran up my arms as the reality of being watched all the time set in.

But Bryan had prepared me for this. With the orbs watching our every move, I wasn't supposed to say or do anything that might anger the faeries or the gods. If I did, they'd have it out for me, and I'd risk them creating competitions that purposefully weren't in my favor.

"The chosen champions are about to enter Vesta's

Villa!" Bacchus said, his voice amplified by the orbs. "But before they do, they'll give us a taste of the magic the gods have gifted them with. We'll go in order of their arrival. Which means Octavia, chosen champion of Neptune—you're up first!" He turned to Octavia and shot her a megawatt grin that was purely meant for the cameras. "Come stand next to me and give the audience a demonstration of your magic!"

33

SELENA

OCTAVIA DROPPED the reins of her horse, stepped out of her chariot, and walked to stand next to Bacchus.

She was only half the size of the giant god, but she held herself in a manner that made me think she could command any room she entered. She wore a stunning deep blue gown that matched her eyes and wings. But despite being dressed up, her expression was fierce and dangerous, like a warrior.

Although that changed a second later, as if she was just remembering not to look like a threat in front of us.

"May I please have some music?" she asked Bacchus sweetly, batting her eyelids as she spoke.

"Of course." He returned her smile and snapped his fingers. There was a burst of light, and then a black and gold instrument appeared out of thin air and floated into his hand. It looked like a mix between a guitar and a harp, and it was huge—clearly meant to be played by a god. "This harp lute was crafted by Apollo," he said proudly, propping his scepter against the chariot so he could hold the instrument with both hands. "Do you have a specific song you want to request?"

Octavia gave him another sweet smile. "Just play something pretty."

"A pretty song for a beautiful girl," he said. "It'll be my pleasure."

But before he could start to play, a girl with long blond hair a few shades darker than mine hopped off her chariot and hurried toward the two of them.

The orbs zoomed in on her, as if asking the question on all of our minds—what was she doing?

"Please excuse me," she said, smiling up at Bacchus and giving him a small curtsy. She wore a teal, Regency style dress that was stunning against her bright yellow wings. "But may I play and sing a song for Octavia? This way, the two of us can demonstrate our gifts at the same time." She gave Octavia a friendly smile, seeming to hope the two of them would become fast friends.

Octavia's lips were set in a firm line, and she glared at the yellow-winged girl in annoyance.

Someone didn't like her spotlight being stolen.

The yellow-winged girl took a step back and lowered

her gaze from Octavia's, as if just now realizing her mistake. But the offer had already been made. Turning back now would make her look scared and weak. An easy target in the Faerie Games.

All she could do was wait for Bacchus to make his decision.

"What a wonderful idea!" Bacchus grinned, looking back and forth between the girls in amusement. "It's fitting that Antonia, the chosen champion of Apollo, should play this unique instrument, handcrafted by her patron god." From the way he looked at the cameras as he said Antonia's name, he was clearly saying her name for the audience's sake, so they'd know who she was. "Here you go, Antonia." He held a hand up and floated the harp lute toward her. It got smaller as it moved, shifting from an instrument meant to be played by a god into one meant to be played by a fae. "I look forward to seeing—and hearing—both of you demonstrating your magic. It's so nice to see friendships forming between this year's champions already."

Antonia sat on the steps and held the harp lute expertly in her hands. She looked to Octavia for a cue to begin.

Octavia remained laser focused on the crowd ahead, her ocean blue eyes storming with anger. The friendliness she'd faked while speaking to Bacchus was gone.

Apparently realizing that Octavia wasn't going to acknowledge her, Antonia took a deep breath and looked out to the crowd. "This is called 'The Last Rose of Summer,'" she said softly, her voice light and musical.

Then, she began to play. Her fingers moved across the strings in a blur, creating a beautiful, haunting tune that entranced me where I stood. Wisps of sparkly yellow magic floated out from her hands and danced around the strings. I felt the music calming every cell of my body, and all I wanted was to relax and listen.

When she sang, her voice was clear and perfect, like an angel.

Octavia looked momentarily entranced, too. But she blinked and got ahold of herself, raising her hands and focusing on the fountain ahead.

A second later, spouts of water burst forth from the fountain, dancing to the melody. It reminded me of clips from movies I'd seen of the Bellagio fountains in Las Vegas. Octavia's hands moved like she was conducting a symphony, and the water followed her commands, dancing in time with the music.

As the song continued, I looked over to Julian. Much to my surprise, his eyes found mine, too. I instantly became aware of every little thing going on in my body —my skin prickling, my breaths deepening, and my heart racing. As crazy as it sounded, I could have sworn his soul was synced with mine.

As the song ended, the water flew up so high that it misted down upon my face.

I pulled my eyes away from Julian's, embarrassed about staring at him for so long. Luckily, everyone seemed too mesmerized by the music to have noticed.

Antonia plucked the final note, and silence descended upon the crowd. I felt like I'd been floating in a dream while listening, and had just now been returned to reality.

The crowd clapped, and I clapped, too, along with all the other chosen champions. I peeked at Julian, but he was focused on Octavia, as if that strange connection between us hadn't happened at all.

But while Julian was no longer looking at me, someone else was. Felix—the one with movie star looks who had been chosen by Venus. His gaze was intense, like he was trying to figure me out. But when my eyes met his, he just gave me a charming smile before turning his focus back to Octavia and Antonia.

I pushed away the uneasy feeling I had from being scrutinized by him, also turning my attention back to the two chosen champions still standing next to Bacchus.

Their performances were just as Bryan had told me

they'd be. Impressive, but not dangerous. Because now wasn't the time to show how useful our magic could be in a fight. Then we'd look like a threat, and that would make us an early target in the Games.

These performances required a delicate balance to appear not threatening but still in control.

"Thank you, ladies," Bacchus said, his strong voice silencing the cheering crowd. Unlike faeries, the rule about owing a favor by saying thank you didn't apply to gods. "Now, return to your chariots. You'll watch the others demonstrate their magic, as they just watched you. And then, once all eleven of you are done showing us what you can do, you'll enter Vesta's Villa and will start getting to know each other."

The last line he spoke had a sinister undertone to it. Because I—and everyone else in the crowd—knew what he meant by "getting to know each other."

It would be time for us to start sizing each other up and forming alliances.

34

SELENA

ONE BY ONE, the chosen champions stepped up next to Bacchus and demonstrated his or her magic.

Molly, the chosen champion of Diana, held out her arms and looked to the sky. Hawks flew down to perch on her arms. So many came down that she was covered in them, from her head all the way to her feet. But suddenly, she was gone, and all the hawks but one flew off, forming the symbol of antlers in the air as they disappeared into the horizon.

Antlers were Diana's symbol. The goddess of animals and the hunt. Her chosen champions could communicate telepathically with animals, as Molly had just demonstrated.

The remaining hawk landed on the ground and shimmered, leaving Molly standing in its place.

Diana's chosen champion could also shift into any animal he or she had ever touched since receiving her magic.

Felix walked up to the first row of the crowd and drove three fae women to such pleasure that they passed out, just from his touch. He looked ridiculously arrogant and full of himself the entire time, as would be expected from the chosen champion of Venus.

Julian pulled three longswords out of thin air and had Bacchus light them aflame. Then he juggled them, throwing them higher than the roof of the villa.

My heart raced, afraid that one of the swords would come down the wrong way and kill him in an instant.

But Julian was chosen by Mars, the god of war. So of course the swords didn't fall. He even added a fourth sword into the mix, and then a fifth, until he was juggling five flaming swords with no difficulty at all.

The crowd held a collective breath, as if worried he might make a mistake at any moment.

He didn't.

Once done, he shoved the tips of all five swords into the ground at his feet. The flames snuffed out and the swords disappeared, steel gray magic exploding up like smoke into the sky.

The crowd burst into applause, hooting and hollering for Julian like crazy.

Cassia, the chosen champion of Ceres, made the buds along the vines surrounding the villa burst into full bloom. Vesta's Villa had been impressive before, but thanks to Cassia, it was a colorful bouquet of beauty.

Ceres was the goddess of agriculture and fertility, and her chosen champions had power over the element of earth, as Cassia had just demonstrated.

The crowd clapped for her, although not nearly as loudly as they had for Julian.

Eventually, all ten of the others had taken their turns and shown off their magic. It was all lighthearted and fun, like we were auditioning for a circus instead of entering a game where we'd connive against each other and fight to the death.

Finally, Bacchus turned to me, a curious glint dancing in his dark, mischievous eyes. "Selena Pearce, chosen champion of Jupiter," he said, nail-biting silence descending upon the crowd as his spoke my patron god's name. "It's only appropriate that we leave the most intriguing player of this year's Games for last." He grinned at me, and while I smiled politely back, I inwardly groaned at how he was bringing extra attention to me. "Come stand by me and give a demonstration of your magic!"

The crowd erupted into applause as I stepped off the chariot and walked toward Bacchus. They clapped for me louder than they'd clapped for any other chosen champion.

I'd expected as much, because Bryan and Finn had prepared me for this. As Jupiter's first ever chosen champion, I was bound to get more attention than the other players.

Which made it extra important for me to not let my magic look threatening.

Remembering my training, I positioned my hair artfully over my shoulders and smiled wide, like I was being presented at a beauty pageant.

Bacchus grinned at me like I was a piece of raw meat about to be thrown into a ring of starving lions.

"Bacchus," I said, bowing my head respectfully. "May I please have a bowl of fruit?"

"A bowl of fruit." He chuckled. "What would the chosen champion of Jupiter need with a bowl of fruit?"

"Provide it for me and I'll show you." I kept my gaze on his, refusing to let his reaction throw me off my game.

"Very well." He waved his hand in the air, there was a flash of light, and a giant bowl of fruit appeared beside him on a pedestal. "Show us what you can do." His smile turned sinister, as if he didn't think I could do much with it at all.

But being mediocre was exactly my plan.

I picked up the fruit on top—a bunch of grapes—and held it up in the air. The strappy dress I wore left my arms bare, so when I called forth my magic and felt it buzz and crackle within me, my arm holding onto the grapes glowed with the lightning that sparked through my veins.

The golden orbs flew a few feet away and recorded my every move, broadcasting my glowing arm on the screens so the entire audience could see.

I released my magic into the grapes, and the entire bunch of them turned to ash in my hands. I let the ash fall around me like snow, purposefully leaving bits of it in my hair and on my dress for dramatic effect.

The crowd clapped politely, as they had for some of the other chosen champions with underwhelming performances. It was just what I was going for.

But at the same time, the disappointment on their faces made my heart drop. It was similar to how my teachers at Avalon Academy had always looked at me whenever I'd tried and failed to produce magic. Like they'd expected more from me, and I'd let them down.

I hated that feeling.

Because I wanted to be more than the powerless girl who couldn't defend herself. And now that Jupiter had gifted me with his magic, I could finally show them all that I was more than a disappointment. I could be strong. I could be powerful.

I could be everything I'd always wanted to be.

Lightning crackled stronger through my veins, bubbling to my skin and glowing brighter as it begged to be released. Anger stormed within me so intensely that I felt powerful enough to make bolts strike down from the sky. I wanted to try to do that, just to see if I could.

But I was supposed to be disintegrating fruit.

So once the claps quieted, I took a deep breath to calm down my magic and reached for the next piece of fruit in the basket—an apple. I held the apple up in the air and did the same thing with it as I had to the bunch of grapes, allowing the ashes of the fruit to collect in my hair and around my feet.

The crowd clapped again, although they sounded less enthused than they had with the grapes. I ignored the murmurs of discontent the best I could and continued using my magic to disintegrate each piece of fruit in the basket.

Finally, I reached the final and largest fruit in there. A watermelon. It was a huge watermelon—probably around the same size as a god's head—so I had to raise it with both hands over my head.

When I looked out to the crowd again, they looked

bored. A few of them even yawned and talked amongst themselves, loudly. It was like they *wanted* me to know that I wasn't interesting enough to deserve their attention for less than five minutes.

The watermelon disintegrated in my hands before I realized I'd let my magic loose.

The ash drifted like snow around me, and all was silent for a few precious seconds.

"That's it?" a large, red-winged fae man finally said from the side of the front row. "Jupiter's champion is disintegrating *fruit?*"

"So disappointing," another fae agreed.

With that, the floodgates opened, and more and more fae voiced their discontent.

"I expected more than that."

"We wanted lightning!"

"She doesn't stand a chance in the Games. She'll be killed off the first week."

"She's useless."

"Better off dead."

"I thought Jupiter's chosen champion would be special. Guess I was wrong."

Their voices erupted around me until I couldn't distinguish one from the other anymore. And the voices weren't the only things spinning around me.

The golden orbs recording every moment of this public embarrassment were having a heyday. Two of them buzzed around my face to broadcast my humiliation for all of the Otherworld to see. The buzzing seeped into every crevice of my brain, until my head felt like it was going to explode.

I just wanted it to *stop*.

So I crossed my arms over my chest like a shield, and the lightning crackling through my veins burst out through my palms. Thick bolts of it shot through the air and struck the orbs hovering around me in a bright flash of blinding light.

A second later, there was ash on the ground below where the orbs had been.

The big screen televisions overhead went dark.

The crowd stared at me in stunned silence.

"You wanted lighting?" I muttered, mostly to myself, but also to them. "Well, there you go. You got your lightning."

The screens lit up again, but I was no longer on the screen. Bacchus was. And the normally jovial god was so livid that his entire face was flushed bright red.

"Selena Peace, chosen champion of Jupiter," he said, my name echoing from the orbs with an impending sense of doom. "You just attacked and destroyed magical equipment created by the gods for use in the Faerie

Games, and are therefore in violation of the rules of the Games."

I gulped and turned around, facing his commanding form. He was terrifying, with his glowing green eyes, red face, and dark wild hair.

"I'm sorry," I forced out, lowering my eyes and praying he accepted my apology. "I got angry, and... I didn't realize what I was doing. I'm sorry."

The words were all coming out wrong. Now it sounded like I couldn't control my magic. Which, technically, was kind of true. But I wasn't supposed to admit it. Especially not in front of the other players.

This was a disaster.

A glance at the other chosen champions showed that most of them were smirking, amused by my massive mistake. A handful of them looked worried, including the chosen champion of Ceres—the bright-eyed girl with green wings who'd made the villa bloom with flowers.

And then there was Julian. He gripped the reins of his horse, his eyes raging with anger. He looked like he was going to charge at Bacchus and thrust a flaming sword through his heart if the god did anything to hurt me.

I had no idea what to make of his reaction. But Julian wasn't what I needed to be worrying about right now.

Because I couldn't just stand there. I needed to try saying *something* else to save myself. Because the punishment for violating the rules of the Games...

The punishment was almost always death.

"It was a mistake." My body shook with fear, but I raised my eyes and met Bacchus's blazing ones. "I'm sorry. I won't do it again. I promise."

His expression flickered from anger to amusement. "Whether I believe you or not isn't important." He leaned against his chariot and toyed with his scepter, resting it across his shoulder. "Because I'm only the host of the Games. Your sentencing falls to the rule maker herself. The queen of the gods—Juno."

35

SELENA

MY HEART DROPPED at the name of Jupiter's jealous
wife.

The goddess who most likely had it out for me and
wanted me dead.

But before I could worry about it any longer, a blue
orb of swirling light appeared at the top of the stairs. It
grew and grew, until it was big enough to hold a god.
Then the light faded until it was gone completely.

In its place, a stunning, dark-haired woman in a blue
and gold dress sat on a throne backed with the feathers
of peacocks. One side of the dress was slit all the way up
to her thigh. She wore gold cuffs on both arms that went
from her wrists to her elbows, and a gleaming gold and
sapphire crown on her head.

She was by far the most beautiful woman I'd ever

seen. But her beauty was harsh and intimidating. Like a warning to everyone to watch their backs.

Juno.

Given what had just happened, I expected her to be looking at me. But she wasn't. Instead, she focused on Bacchus, her stone gaze cold enough to make the giant god shrink in her presence.

"Your magic shouldn't have been able to be destroyed by a half-blood." She held her chin high, looking down at Bacchus like he was lower than dirt. "Even a half-blood gifted with magic from a god."

The corner of Bacchus's mouth twitched in annoyance. "You're right." He gave me a lethal glare before returning his focus to Juno. "I was as shocked as everyone else when she did what she did. But my father's magic is strong. Apparently that strength transferred to the half-blood when he chose her as his champion."

Juno's eyes narrowed as he spoke, as if she couldn't stand the sound of his voice. "My husband's magic *is* strong," she said. "It amused me to watch the half-blood he chose for the Games destroy your magic so easily."

Bacchus's hand tightened around his scepter at her venomous words.

I blinked, looking back and forth between the two of them as I put the pieces together. Because if I understood correctly from what they'd just said, Jupiter was both Juno's husband *and* Bacchus's father.

And judging from the way Juno looked at Bacchus with so much hatred, I guessed that not only was she not his mother, but she had it out for him big time.

Fascinating. Especially because if she was amused by my accidental stint, perhaps there was hope for me yet.

Apparently done with scolding Bacchus, Juno turned her hawkish gaze straight at me. "Selena Pearce," she said my name with disdain. "Aren't you a pretty little thing."

From the way she said it, it clearly wasn't a compliment. And now she was silent, staring at me, waiting for me to say something.

I swallowed and mustered up the courage to speak. "Your Highness." I dipped into a low curtsy before turning my gaze up to hers again. I wasn't sure if that was how I was supposed to address a goddess, but since her expression remained unchanged, it didn't seem like she hated it. That was good. At least, I thought it was. "I'm sorry for breaking the orbs. I didn't mean to do it."

I'd technically done more than broken them. I'd disintegrated them. But it was the same thing. Kind of.

"You might not have meant to do it, but you still did it." She tilted her head curiously. "Why?"

From the challenge in her sharp eyes, I knew not to mess this one up.

But there was no lie I could invent to explain what I'd done. And Devyn had told me that no matter what happened in the Games, I should follow my gut.

Which meant telling Juno the truth.

"Until Jupiter gifted me with his magic, I had no magic of my own." I shifted in place, since making myself vulnerable with so many eyes on me was uncomfortable. Especially since the golden orbs were buzzing around me again, broadcasting me so all the fae could hear.

But I'd do whatever it took to stay alive. So if a confession was what they wanted, then that was what they'd get.

"All my life I've been powerless," I continued, gaining confidence as I spoke. "Helpless. Weak. I was a disappointment to everyone around me, and I hated it. Now, I finally have my own magic. But the crowd was disappointed with my demonstration of it. They started calling me all those things I spent my entire life hating about myself. They wouldn't stop. And I just... well, I got angry."

"You got so angry that you disintegrated Bacchus's magical orbs with bolts of lightning."

When she put it like that, it sounded pretty crazy.

"The orbs were buzzing in my ears, and it felt like they were mocking me, too." I shrugged, continuing before she could respond. "I'm sorry. I promise it won't happen again. Just give me the chance to continue in the Games. Please."

"And why should I do that?"

"Because as the first champion ever chosen by Jupiter, I'm still discovering what I can do." Determination rose in me as I held her gaze, refusing to back down. "It's a learning process. But it'll be entertaining to watch. Don't you think?"

The words shocked me the moment they came out of my mouth. Because I never thought I'd be begging to be *in* the Faerie Games.

Now here I was, doing just that.

It was funny how the threat of sudden death could result in such desperate measures.

Well, it *would* be funny, if it wasn't completely terrifying. Especially since Bacchus was glowering at me like he wanted to smite me on the spot himself.

So much for trying not to anger the gods. I was already failing at the Games, and we hadn't even entered the villa yet.

Juno glanced at Bacchus, smirked, and turned back to me. "It was rather entertaining," she said, moving her focus farther ahead, to the attentive crowd gathered before us. "Don't you all think it was entertaining?"

The faeries in the crowd exploded with applause. They clapped and screamed louder than they had for any of the other chosen champions. They were so loud that I could *feel* the vibration of their excitement all over my skin.

Juno let the cheering go on for what felt like minutes.

With my life on the line, they were the longest few minutes ever.

Finally, Juno raised her hand, and the crowd silenced. "This half-blood doesn't seem like anything special to me," she said. "But my husband chose her as his champion for a reason. So despite her transgression, Selena Pearce will be allowed to play in the Faerie Games." She turned back to me, staring down at me like a falcon eyeing its prey. "I look forward to watching you try to show me—and everyone else in the Otherworld— what you're made of. That is, *if* you're truly made of anything at all."

A massive weight lifted from my shoulders. All at once, I could breathe again. The world around me became sharper, clearer.

It didn't matter that the queen of the gods had just insulted me in front of everyone. Because I had a second chance. And I wasn't going to mess it up.

"Thank you, Your Highness." I smiled sweetly, giving her another polite curtsy. "I'll do my best not to let you down."

Outwardly, I remained calm. But adrenaline coursed through my veins, and I was more ramped up than ever.

Juno might think I was "nothing special."

But I couldn't wait to show her—and everyone else in the Otherworld—how wrong they were.

SELENA

JUNO DISAPPEARED in an orb of swirling light as quickly as she'd arrived.

With her gone, Bacchus stood straighter and held his scepter strong beside him. "Well, that was an exciting ceremony!" he said, back to his upbeat, loud self. "Now, the chosen champions will enter Vesta's Villa in the order they arrived. And once they're all inside... let the Faerie Games begin!"

The crowd erupted in applause again. And just as instructed, the other players stepped off their chariots and lined up in front of the wide stone steps.

Octavia glared at me, like she didn't think I deserved to be there. Julian gave me a single nod—of respect, it seemed like—although he looked away a moment later. The others didn't acknowledge me at all.

I took my spot as the last person in line. Once I was there, Bacchus slammed his scepter against the ground. The giant doors to the villa swung open, and Octavia led the way inside.

Upon entering Vesta's Villa, I looked around in awe. The ceilings were high, both them and the walls engraved with intricate patterns of vines and flowers. A sparkling, crystal chandelier hung from the ceiling. Gold-framed artwork lined the walls, each one a portrait of a fae. Although when I got closer to one of the paintings, I noticed that the man portrayed in it wore fake silver tips on his ears, similar to the golden ones Bryan had put on my ears this morning.

He was a chosen champion. And not just *any* chosen champion.

The plaque on the bottom of the frame said: *Hugh Flanagan, Chosen Champion of Neptune, Winner of the Faerie Games, Year 497 AD.*

Someone moved to stand next to me, watching me examine the portrait.

It was Bridget, a girl with gleaming gold wings, sharp features, and blue eyes lacking so much pigment that they appeared gray. She was Minerva's chosen champion. Bridget could see the future, which she'd demonstrated earlier by accurately predicting what number would fall when we all rolled a dice, and what cards we would pull from a deck Bacchus supplied for her.

"Do you know him?" She motioned to the man in the painting.

One of the golden orbs that had followed us into the villa zoomed over, buzzing around us. But I did my best to ignore it.

If I ignored the orb, I was less likely to get irritated at it and do something rash, like disintegrate it with lightning.

"I don't know him." I chuckled, although her question wasn't completely ridiculous, since half-bloods became immortal the moment we were chosen by a god. "Is there a portrait in the villa for every winner of the Games?"

"Yes," she said. "Over fifteen hundred of them."

That explained why the walls were covered in portraits. "When exactly did the Faerie Games start?" I asked, since she seemed like the type of person who'd know the answer.

"The Faerie Games started in 476 AD." She stuck her nose in the air, as if I should already know this. "The year Romulus Augustulus, the last Emperor of Rome, was killed by the demon Odoacer."

I snapped my gaze away from the portrait to look at

her. "You mean a *demon* was responsible for the fall of the Roman Empire?"

"Of course." She scoffed. "Odaecer wanted to be king, and he allied with dark witches to make it happen. But he feared the fae, so he worked with the witches to create the spell that made all fae allergic to iron. After the spell took hold, the fae couldn't live on Earth anymore, so they retreated back to the Otherworld. But even though they had to retreat, they wanted to continue the culture they'd loved on Earth—the Roman Empire. And with that, the Faerie Games began."

"Not much is known about the fae on Earth or Avalon," I explained, since I didn't want Bridget to think I was dumb for not knowing this important piece of history. "There are stories, of course. But all written history of the fae was destroyed centuries ago."

She studied me and nodded, as if accepting my explanation. "That makes sense, since civilizations on Earth plunged into the Dark Ages after the fae retreated back to the Otherworld," she said. "No one realized what a positive impact the fae had on Earth until they were gone and cursed to never return. A lot was lost in those centuries."

"You know a lot about the history of the fae," I said, already sizing her up. Because if she knew as much as she seemed to know—especially if that knowledge extended to what had worked and what hadn't worked in previous Faerie Games—she could be a good ally.

"I love history—especially war history." She gave me a sly smile. "Minerva chose me as her champion for a reason."

From the hungry way she was looking at me, I had a feeling she was considering me as an ally, too.

But before I could respond, the giant fireplace on the other side of the room lit ablaze. The fire was so hot and bright that all eleven of us turned to look at it at once.

The fire popped, and a beautiful woman in a flowing orange gown stepped out of the flames. She wore a stunning gold necklace and a matching headpiece with pearls that dropped over her forehead. Her eyes were such a light brown that they were basically orange, like fire.

The flames continued burning behind her, although not as intensely as before.

"I'm Vesta, goddess of the hearth and the home," she said, her voice warm and soothing. "Welcome to my villa. I can't wait to get to know each and every one of you." She looked around, meeting each of our gazes.

When she reached me, she paused for a second longer than she had for everyone else. Her eyes gleamed brighter with intrigue. But then she looked away, focusing on the group as a whole once more.

"To ease into the introductions, a feast has been prepared and is waiting for us in the dining room," she continued. "It's time to break bread together and celebrate the start of this year's Faerie Games."

SELENA

MOST EVERYONE SCRAMBLED after Vesta as she led the way to the dining room.

Octavia knocked into my shoulder as she shoved her way past me. "Watch it." She glared at me before continuing to push forward until she was right behind Vesta.

She clearly had it out for me already. I needed to keep an eye on her.

It didn't take long to reach the dining room, which was just as elegant as the foyer. Like in the foyer, the walls were covered with portraits of previous winners of the Games. A beautiful marble fireplace along the interior wall already burned with warm, crackling flames. On the other wall was a large window providing a breathtaking view of the flowering gardens. But the gardens were surrounded with hedges that looked to be twenty feet tall—like they were keeping us in as much as they were keeping the general public out.

A long dining table made of polished wood sat in the center of the room, with twelve chairs around it. It was set with delicate chinaware, and in the center was an overflowing abundance of meats, cheeses, fruits, juices, and wine. The smell of all the food made my mouth water. But only one chair was at the head of the table. The rest were along the sides, although unevenly, with five on one side and six on the other.

The golden orbs followed us into the dining room, buzzing above our heads.

Vesta walked to the chair at the head of the table and placed her hand on the top of it. "Please seat yourselves," she said. "I imagine you're all hungry after your impressive performances in the magic demonstration ceremony."

This time I *definitely* didn't imagine that she looked at me for slightly longer than she looked at any of the others.

The extra attention I was getting from being Jupiter's first chosen champion was already getting old, and the Games had barely begun.

Octavia, Bridget, Felix, and Antonia rushed to grab seats near Vesta before anyone else had a chance. Most of the others followed suit, until only three of us remained. Cassia, Julian, and me.

I walked with them to the three seats at the far end of the table.

Julian claimed his seat first—the one with another seat next to him. He looked at me steadily, as if daring me to sit next to him.

I ached to do just that. The thought of being near him gave me a rush of comfort that I couldn't explain.

But my feelings were betraying me. I shouldn't want to be near Julian. He was the forbidden fruit, and as much as I wanted to take another bite, I also knew that would be a terrible idea.

So I pushed my feelings for him away, burying them deep down inside myself where they belonged. And instead of sitting next to him, I hurried to the seat across from him before I could change my mind.

Once I sat down, I realized my mistake. Because it was going to be impossible to keep myself from looking across the table at Julian throughout the meal.

How had it only been a week ago that his lips had kissed mine? So much had happened since then. The person I'd been when I'd kissed him felt worlds away from the person I was now.

His lips curled into a knowing smirk, and the moment I met his amused ice blue eyes, I knew he'd noticed me staring at him. My cheeks heated with embarrassment.

I needed to get my focus where it belonged, which was anywhere *but* on Julian. If I couldn't manage that, then this was going to be one torturously long meal.

No—it was going to be a torturously long competition.

Especially since only one of us could get out of it alive.

With Juno nearly sentencing me to death, the Games felt more real than ever. Before, I was holding out hope that my parents and their army would rescue me and put an end to this. But even though it was still a possibility, I couldn't have that attitude anymore.

Which meant treating the Games like I was playing until the end.

And like Bryan had said, I could make it to the final three without killing anyone. Once I was there, I'd have no choice—it was either kill or be killed. But until then, I didn't want to kill anyone if I didn't have to.

I needed to play the best social game I could to get as little blood on my hands as possible.

"Before we eat, I want to explain my role in the Games," Vesta said from her seat at the head of the table. "I'm the 'house mother.' I'll provide you with food and drinks, like this lovely feast I've readied today. If you need anything specifically, ask me and I'll decide whether or not to give it to you. Most importantly, I know life is difficult for chosen champions in the villa, because in the Faerie Games, no one truly knows who they can trust. So if you need an unbiased party to talk to, you can come to my private quarters. Everything we discuss in there won't be repeated to the other players in the Game.

"But I can't tell you what moves you should make," she continued. "In our conversations, I'll help you think through the pros and cons for the options you have. What you decide to do from there is up to you, and you alone."

Having an unbiased confidant inside the Games sounded too good to be true.

When things sounded too good to be true, it usually meant they were.

I'd have to watch what I discussed with Vesta. Because sure, she seemed nice and caring. But she was still one of the gods.

I didn't trust the gods. We were pawns to them— nothing more.

"There's one final rule you need to know, and then we can eat." She eyed the food, like she was hungry, too. Did gods even get hungry? I wasn't sure. "You're not allowed to use your magic to physically injure other players inside the villa, or on its grounds. If you do, you'll be eliminated from the Games immediately."

"Good." Octavia scoffed. "Since Jupiter's player can't control her powers, it sounds like she'll get herself eliminated on her own. Like what *should* have happened when she broke the rules by attacking the orbs." She glared at me so intensely that her hatred was like a living, breathing thing.

An orb buzzed closer to me, apparently waiting to broadcast my reaction to everyone watching this go down.

"Juno created the rules of the Games." I spoke calmly, despite the storm brewing within myself from the anger at Octavia's calling me out in front of everyone. "What 'should' happen is whatever she decides. And she decided to let me play." I held Octavia's gaze, daring her to argue any differently when we both knew that all the gods—including Juno—were watching our every move.

Juno didn't seem like the type of woman who'd appreciate a half-blood telling her they disagreed with her decision.

Octavia must have thought the same thing, because she grabbed her knife, braced it on top of the table, and glared at me. "You better watch your back, Blondie," she snarled. "Because I'm coming for you."

My heart stopped in my chest.

But I couldn't let Octavia see that she'd intimidated me. So I took a deep breath and got ahold of myself.

"Game on," I said coolly, and then I checked my nails, as if they were far more important than anything else Octavia could say to me.

The orbs glowed brighter and buzzed louder, as if the drama entertained them.

Vesta brought her hands together in a dramatic fashion and looked back and forth between Octavia and me. "This has been an eventful start to the feast," she said brightly, looking at the rest of the players sitting quietly around the table. "Does anyone else have any grievances they wish to air at this time?"

A few of them eyed others, but no one said a word.

I focused on the plate in front of me. No need to bring any *more* attention to myself after all the events of today.

"Wonderful." Vesta smiled, although her smile didn't look genuine. The Games were truly on, and I couldn't trust anyone—not even our house mother. "In that case, let's eat."

SELENA

AFTER DINNER, we retreated to the library with our glasses of juice or wine. Most of the players—myself included—chose juice. According to Bryan, Devyn was just being a jerk during our first breakfast together when he implied that faeries only drank wine. Juice was perfectly acceptable, too.

One of the mantras of the Faerie Games was to expect anything at any time, and to always watch your back. So it was smart to stay sober.

The library, like all the other rooms I'd seen in the villa so far, was gorgeous. Books lined the shelves, and portraits were displayed on the walls between them. A crystal chandelier hung from the engraved ceiling, a plush Turkish rug cushioned my feet, and big comfy chairs sat in the center of the room, facing each other so people could chat around the blazing fireplace.

Octavia commanded the center of the room, instantly befriending the other chosen champions.

After the scene at the dining room table, it was my best move to lay low for a while. And so, drawn to the books, I walked over to the biggest shelf and ran my fingers across the soft leather spines.

Reading had always been one of my favorite things to do back on Avalon. Books allowed me to escape my life where I never truly fit in, and they gave me the opportunity to live in the minds of so many different people. Despite having never left my home until last week, I felt like I'd visited so many places and so many times, all thanks to the magic contained in the pages of books.

I browsed the titles of the spines, reaching for one that sounded interesting.

It didn't budge.

I pulled harder, but it still didn't move. It was like it was superglued in place.

"We can't access the books," someone said from next to me. Cassia, the chosen champion of Ceres. She was soft-spoken and had a sweet look to her, thanks to her round, pink cheeks. "We're not allowed to read during the Games."

"Why not?" I asked.

"Because it would be boring to the viewers if we sat around reading all day." She glanced at the orb buzzing around us, broadcasting our every move. "They want us to talk to each other. The more we talk to each other, the more likely we are to stir up drama. So there's a spell cast over the books so we can't touch them."

I nodded, since it made sense, although I was bummed I wouldn't be able to read. "I don't think I've ever gone a few days without reading," I said, giving a final longing look at the untouchable books beside me.

"Me, too," she said. "No matter how tired I was after work, I always fit in an extra fifteen minutes or so before bed to read." She smiled, and I had an instant feeling that we could be friends.

It was a shame that by the end of the Games, one—or both—of us would be dead.

But I couldn't let my mind go there. If I did, I doubted I'd be able to escape the endless loop of fear that threatened to take hold at any second.

I needed to take this one step at a time. My focus had to be on getting allies. Cassia seemed open to doing just that. And since she was the only other player interested in talking to me—the rest were flocking to Octavia and a few other strong looking champions in the center of the room—I needed to take this opportunity and roll with it.

"I don't think we've been properly introduced yet," I said with what I hoped was a smile as warm as hers. "I'm Selena."

"Cassia," she said, although of course I already knew that.

We both raised our glasses in a toast, as if acknowledging the friendship forming between us.

It was amazing how a mutual love of reading could instantly bring people together.

"Your performance in the opening ceremony was impressive," I said. "I've always loved flowers. We had a ton of them back where I'm from."

"Are you from Earth?" She lowered her voice slightly when she said "Earth," like it was a scandalous thing to talk about.

"Sort of," I said. "I'm from Avalon—an anchor island connected to Earth. The island is technically in a realm of its own, but being anchored to Earth makes it easy for people living on the island to go back and forth as they please."

"Fascinating," she said. "We don't know anything about Avalon here in the Otherworld."

"Probably because Avalon was created after the fae left Earth," I said, remembering what Bridget had said about the fae retreating back to the Otherworld in the fifth century AD. "The island was created in the sixth century—during King Arthur's time. Although no one actually lived there until a little over sixteen years ago, when my parents turned it into what it is today."

"But I thought Prince Devyn was your father?" she asked.

"Prince Devyn and I barely know each other." I glanced at the orb buzzing around us, hoping Devyn was watching me reject him in front of the entire Otherworld. "My real parents are Queen Annika and Prince Jacen, the founders of Avalon and the leaders of the Nephilim army." My parents never used their royal titles, but the fae seemed impressed by titles, so I made sure to use them now. "They took me in after I was born. They raised me, and that makes them my true parents."

Cassia nodded, although she glanced warily at the orb. I understood why. It would be dangerous for her to say anything negative about the fae when they were listening in.

It was probably dangerous for me, too. But I didn't care. I wanted the entire Otherworld to know about my parents and how powerful they were.

They needed to know what was coming for them.

"I want to learn more about this place you're from—

Avalon." Cassia's eyes glowed with excitement as she spoke the name of my home. "Here in the Otherworld, we don't know much of anything about the other realms. Or at least, the half-bloods don't."

"I'll tell you everything." I leaned forward, as if sharing a juicy secret. "But I want to learn everything you know about the Otherworld in return."

The more I knew, the more I could be ready for anything this realm threw my way.

"Deal." She smiled. "I suppose that while we might not have books, we can still tell each other stories. And that's almost as good."

"Almost," I agreed, since I could tell that like me, she thought nothing compared to the joy of reading.

Suddenly, someone moved away from the group in the center and toward the two of us. Tall, pink wings, and movie star handsome.

Felix.

"Ladies." He shot us a winning grin, and his teeth were so white that I could almost swear they *sparkled*. "Why are the two most beautiful chosen champions hiding away in the corner of the room?"

"We're not hiding." Cassia looked up at Felix with eyes as round as saucers. "We were just getting to know each other."

He pressed his hand against the bookshelf and leaned

forward, like he was trapping her in a cage.

She smiled dreamily up at him, loving being close to him. It was like she was hypnotized.

"Do you want to get to know me, too?" he asked, his voice low and seductive.

It sounded so corny I had to stop myself from gagging.

"I'd love that," she said, and even though half-bloods could lie, I could tell she meant it. "Wouldn't you, Selena?"

I didn't get it. Sure, Felix was attractive. Someone would have to be blind not to see that. But he seemed so sleazy. How was Cassia captivated by his "charms" so easily?

I certainly wasn't.

But the Games were just starting. It was too early to make enemies. So I needed to play nice.

For now.

"Sure," I said, although I stepped back from Felix. He was trying to state his dominance by towering over us, and I didn't like it.

He tilted his head and studied me quizzically, as if I'd said something wrong.

Could he tell that his charm—which had to be part of his magic—wasn't working on me?

I had no way of knowing if that were the case. But if

it were, I didn't want him to know.

If he didn't know, I could use it against him later.

"I mean yes," I corrected myself, throwing in a sugary sweet smile for good measure. "I'd love that, too."

He nodded, apparently pleased by my change in tone. "I see why Jupiter chose you as his champion." His pupils dilated as he gazed down at me, so intense that he looked utterly captivated by my presence. "You're a fascinating creature."

I flinched and backed away, like he was a snake trying to bite me. "Did you really just call me a 'creature?'"

Who did he think he was? God's gift to every female in the universe?

Well, since he was Venus's chosen champion, I supposed that was *exactly* what he was. And while I didn't know why his charm magic wasn't working on me, I was grateful for it.

"Apologies," he said, although his clenched jaw gave away his inner frustration. "You have me so entranced that my words are coming out all wrong."

For some reason, I highly doubted that.

But just then, the last person I expected to join our little circle came walking over, giving Felix an icy stare of death.

Julian.

SELENA

I FROZE in Julian's presence. It was the way I thought Felix had expected me to react to him. But as long as Julian was around, I was convinced that all other guys would just blend into the background.

"Selena," Julian said my name with familiarity and moved to stand closer to me. "It looks like you're settling in well." He gave Felix another death stare, like he was telling him to back off his girl.

I'd seen shifters on Avalon behave this same way after imprinting on a potential mate.

The only problem here was that I *wasn't* Julian's girl. And we certainly hadn't imprinted on each other. That was a shifter thing, not a fae thing.

But I needed to refocus on the conversation. Settling into the villa. Right.

"I am." I steadied myself, refusing to look weak around Julian. Especially since after kissing him in LA, being around him made me feel bare and exposed, like I'd given him a part of myself I could never get back. "Cassia, Felix, and I were just getting to know each other."

Julian glanced over at Cassia, as if just now noticing her. "Sorry for interrupting," he said. "But I've had something I've been wanting to ask Selena, and this is the first moment I've had a chance to speak to her."

Cassia raised an eyebrow, looking back and forth between Julian and me with intrigue. "We'll leave the two of you alone then." She stepped back to go elsewhere, touching Felix's arm to get him to go with her.

"No need to do that." Julian's hard tone stopped her in her tracks. "It won't take long." He focused on Felix again, as if daring him to stay and listen.

What was going on between the two guys? Because the longer I watched, it truly seemed like Julian was behaving like a shifter who'd imprinted.

But Julian only cared about one person—himself. He'd proven it after the way he'd tricked me.

Perhaps there was some past beef between Julian and Felix that I didn't know about.

"Cool." Felix met Julian's gaze with pure confidence,

as if accepting his challenge. "Because Selena and I were enjoying getting to know each other."

I couldn't help it—I rolled my eyes. Because *ew*. If Felix thought I was enjoying getting to know him, he was delusional. Or I was a better actress than I realized.

Julian turned to me, and from the way he looked at me, it felt like we were the only two people in the room. My breath caught, taken off guard by his intense ice blue gaze. "I keep thinking about the time we spent together on Earth," he started, his voice low and hypnotizing. Just the sound of it cast a spell on me. "When we were eating ice cream."

I watched him coldly, since the last thing I wanted to think about was all the lies he'd told me during our date.

The person I'd thought he was didn't exist.

The sooner I could accept that, the sooner I could stop feeling like every cell in my body was urging me closer whenever he was near me.

"Do you remember our conversation?" He looked at me like the world depended on my answer.

"Of course I do," I said quickly, purposefully *not* replaying the conversation in my head. I didn't need to torture myself like that.

"Good." He nodded, although he still looked troubled. Like he could feel the wall I was putting up between us, and he wanted to break it down. "There's something I've been wondering, and I haven't stopping thinking about it since that night. So I figured I'd ask you now." He ran his hand through his dark blond hair, looking nervous. Then he refocused on me and asked, "What did you wish for?"

I jumped back slightly, since I hadn't expected him to ask me that.

Then I thought back to my wish.

I wish I'll get to continue seeing Julian after tonight.

I took a sharp breath inward at the irony of it all, since my wish *had* come true. Just not in the way I'd expected.

It was like the universe was playing a cruel trick on me.

"Aren't wishes supposed to stay secret?" I asked, since there was no way I was giving in and answering his question.

"No." His eyes burned into mine, so intensely that it was like he could see straight into my soul. "Especially if they've already come true."

"I'm not going to tell you." I stood my ground, unwilling to give into him even though my heart urged me otherwise. "Especially because I know you'll never tell me yours."

"That's not true." His eyes flashed with hurt. "To

prove it, I'll tell you right now. My wish was that you'd find it in your heart to forgive me."

I stared up at him for a few more seconds, battling with my conflicting emotions. Because my heart *did* want to forgive him.

But my brain told me that would be naive.

If I wanted to survive the Faerie Games, I couldn't be naive. Which meant controlling my feelings for Julian. If I let my feelings take over—which I knew they would, if I let them—I risked getting distracted from my ultimate goal. Winning the Faerie Games.

And since only one of us could get out alive, giving into my feelings and falling for him was a terrible idea.

Cassia backed away, twisting her fingers around the stem of her glass. "I'm going to get some more juice," she said brightly, forcing a smile. "Felix, are you coming?" She gave Felix a look that clearly said he needed to follow her lead and go with her.

Panic rushed through me. They couldn't leave me alone with Julian.

"I'll go with you." I downed the final sips of my juice, giving Cassia a sharp look that meant she should wait for me. Then I took a deep breath, composed myself, and turned back to Julian. "I'll never forgive you," I said, each word like a stab to my heart as I forced it out. "And I won't tell you my wish."

From the pained way he looked at me, I could tell he felt like he'd been stabbed in the heart, too.

But it was an act. It *had* to be an act. Anything else meant his feelings for me were real.

I shook the thought away. My emotions were deceiving me. I was trying to believe what I *wanted* to be real instead of what was *actually* real. And that would only get me into trouble.

Worse—it would get me killed.

"Felix." I placed my hand on his arm and gave him a flirtatious smile, batting my eyelashes for extra measure. "Do you want to come with us to get more juice?"

Felix smiled down at me, like he'd won whatever game the guys were playing. "Of course." He linked his arm with mine, giving Julian a wolfish grin before returning his undivided attention to me. "It will be my pleasure."

I didn't look back at Julian as the three of us walked away.

Because I knew deep within myself that I'd hurt him on a level I didn't fully understand. I knew because walking away from him hurt me, too.

And if I saw that grief on his face, I worried I'd stop listening to my brain, and give into my traitorous heart.

SELENA

THE MOMENT CASSIA, Felix, and I returned from getting drinks, a bunch of the orbs grouped together to create a large golden sphere above the fireplace. It was about the same size as an average television. A few of the small orbs continued buzzing around us to record us, but the majority of them were now part of the sphere.

The sphere pulsed with light, and an image of Bacchus reclining on a chaise lounge appeared on the "screen." He wore a purple toga that cut across his chest, and a wreath of leaves and grapes on his head. A bunch of grapes sat on a golden plate by his side, and he held a matching golden goblet that I assumed was full of wine.

"Champions!" he said, raising his goblet in a toast. "Please take a seat around the fireplace."

We all walked over and situated ourselves in the

chairs. Octavia sat in the center, surrounded by her new friends. Julian sat near the end with Antonia and Bridget. I led the way to the only remaining seats—the ones across from Julian. Felix and Cassia followed at my heels.

Vesta stood off to the side of the room. No orbs circled anywhere near her.

Bacchus looked us over once we were all seated. "I trust you're finding the villa comfortable?" he asked.

The majority of the players chorused a resounding yes.

Once it was quiet again, Octavia sat straighter and arranged her hair in front of her shoulders. "The villa is lovelier in person than it looked on the orbs," she said with a winning smile. "And the welcome feast was delicious."

What a suck-up. It took all of my self-control not to roll my eyes.

"The feast was certainly entertaining to watch." Bacchus laughed and popped a grape into his mouth. Once he chewed and swallowed, he continued, "And I hope you got your fill of food and drinks during the feast. You're going to need it. Because the first competition starts now."

My mouth nearly dropped open. The other players looked as shocked as I felt.

Bryan and Finn hadn't prepared me for this. In all past Faerie Games, the players had at least one night in the villa before the first competition took place. It allowed us time to get to know each other and form alliances.

No official alliances had formed yet. At least not any that I knew of.

Which meant for this competition, we'd each be on our own.

"I know this is a first," Bacchus continued, quieting the murmurs that had started among us. "But this is also the first time we've had eleven players at the start of the Games. And not including the bed in the Emperor's suite, there are only ten beds in the villa. We couldn't have one of you sleeping on the floor tonight, could we?" He laughed this off as ridiculous, raising his wine glass in jest.

As if sleeping on the floor was the worst of our problems.

"The solution is simple," he continued. "We'll hold the first Emperor of the Villa competition now, so the Emperor of the Week can move into his or her suite tonight." He smiled wickedly, clearly entertained by this curve ball he'd thrown at us. "From there, the week will proceed as planned. The Emperor of the Villa will choose three champions to send to the Coliseum. At the end of the week, those three champions will fight in the arena until one of them is dead. Simple enough, right?"

My stomach knotted in disgust. Because none of this was simple.

It was brutal and twisted.

"Now, I want you all to stand up and give me a twirl," he instructed.

Octavia was the first to stand. When she twirled, her long, ocean blue gown transformed into a short, skirted fighting outfit with matching thigh-high boots. When the red-winged guy next to her spun, his elegant tunic shifted into a plainer one belted at the waist, his breeches tucked into flat boots that went mid-way up his calves.

The rest of us followed suit, our formal wear also changing into fighting gear. I wore the same light blue mini dress Bryan had me practice in while training in Devyn's house.

"What a fierce group of champions." Bacchus eyed us appreciatively. "Your stylists were told about the first competition being today, so they could cast the appropriate spell on your formal wear. They were also placed under a charm so they wouldn't reveal the secret to you. Because what fun would it be if the secret was spilled early?" He laughed again, clearly entertained by himself.

Most of the other players laughed along, as if Bacchus was the wittiest god in the universe.

Of course they did.

I had to remember that the Games were rigged. It was in our best interest to make sure the gods liked us.

So I threw in a laugh of my own, although I would have bet my eyes looked as hollow and empty as I felt inside.

"Now, for the rules!" Bacchus rose his goblet with so much force that wine splashed over the rim, and we all sat down to listen. "The golden emperor wreath is hidden within the walls of the citadel. To learn its location, you'll go to the main forum in the capital city. There will be signs on the road to direct you there. You can either use the transportation waiting for you outside of the villa, or go by foot. In the forum, you'll receive instructions for where to go to find the wreath."

"Will the instructions be hidden?" Antonia asked, her forehead creased with worry.

"The instructions will be apparent once you arrive in the forum," Bacchus said. "And remember—this is an Emperor of the Villa competition. Injure the other players all you want, but you're not in the arena yet. Which means no killing allowed. And like all competitions in the Games, harming any fae or half-bloods is prohibited. Break these rules, and your fate will be in

Juno's hands." He glanced at me, scowling. "The queen of the gods is rarely as merciful as she was this morning." He paused for a few seconds to let that sink in, then leaned forward and looked over all of us with giddy anticipation. "Now, stand up and follow Vesta to the entrance hall. Once she opens the front doors, the Emperor of the Villa competition will begin!"

41

SELENA

I TREMBLED as we made our way to the entrance hall, although I held my head high, focusing on putting one foot in front of the other. The others were only a muffled buzz in the background.

Because this was it. The first competition.

The Faerie Games suddenly felt more real than ever.

"Any injuries sustained during this competition will heal once one of you claims the wreath." Vesta said once we were all gathered in the entrance hall. "Are there any questions about the rules?"

No one said a word.

Were they as anxious as I was?

Looking around, it didn't seem like it. Bridget stood in front, confident and prepared. Octavia stood in fighting stance, eager to demolish anyone in her way.

Felix was off to the side, way too calm and relaxed given the situation. Julian focused on the doors, his eyes hard, ready for battle.

Cassia stood next to me, and she gave me a nod of encouragement. My nerves calmed slightly. Even though there was no official alliance between the two of us, I trusted that we had each other's back.

Except Bryan and Finn had specifically told me what to do in the first competition.

I wasn't supposed to win.

The first Emperor of the Villa ended up with a target on his or her back once the week was over, because the two players who survived the battle in the arena—and their alliance members—were gunning for them. And while the first Emperor of the Villa could go far in the Games by making a strong alliance from the start, he or she usually never won.

Get selected for the weekly arena battles too many times in a row, and you were bound to lose one of them, no matter how great of a fighter you were.

I was supposed to befriend this week's Emperor of the Villa and grab a spot in his or her alliance. But I wasn't supposed to *be* the Emperor of the Villa. It was too early in the Games to get blood on my hands.

But I still had to try in the competition. I needed to land in the middle of the pack. I couldn't look *so* strong that I was a threat, but I also couldn't look so weak that I was unwanted in an alliance.

I could do this.

I *had* to do this.

What if I helped Cassia win the wreath? I doubted she'd nominate me for the arena fight. She seemed genuine. I truly did trust her.

Prince Devyn had told me to trust my gut. So I gave Cassia a reassuring smile, and by the way she returned it, I knew an unspoken alliance had formed between us.

"I wish you all the best of luck," Vesta said warmly. "I'll see you again once the Emperor of the Villa has been crowned."

She raised her hands, and the double doors swung open.

Six tan horses with flowers woven through their manes and tails were scattered in the front yard. None of them were saddled.

Looked like we'd be riding bareback.

Bridget moved like a bullet, zooming down the steps and leaping onto the closest horse's back. She kicked her heels into her horse's sides and left us in the dust.

Some champions chosen by Minerva had super-speed. Apparently Bridget was one of them. Good to know.

The rest of us ran toward the horses, although not as

fast as Bridget. Except for Molly. hawk, landed on another horse's back, s. her natural form, and took off in a heartbeat.

But why had Bridget and Molly taken horses Bridget's super-speed, she could run just as fast— perhaps faster—than a horse. Molly could shift into a horse, or into an animal that ran faster than a horse.

The answer hit me a second later. Because there were six horses and eleven of us. The five of us who didn't get a horse would have to travel by foot, which would be a massive disadvantage in the competition.

Bridget and Molly had taken horses so two champions would have less of a chance at winning the wreath.

Now there were nine of us left, and four horses remaining.

All hell broke loose as players ran for the horses. The gold orbs zoomed around us. Everyone had someone on their heels except for Cillian—Pluto's chosen champion.

Bryan and Finn had warned me that everyone would be afraid of Cillian. Pluto rarely chose a champion, and those he chose veered toward being psychopathic. Gifted with magic over metal and stones, Pluto's champions won a high percentage of Games they played in. So people didn't want to mess with his champions,

GAMES

She shifted into a

shifted back into

With

or

:tle against them in the

ᴈ and left us in his dust.

son for themselves. And I

by getting shut out of the

gate.

ᴦ own.

ere, a blast of water smacked me from behind. It kn.. :ed me to the ground with so much force that the wind whooshed out of my chest. The water splashed around me, and I was drowning in it, unable to breathe. Pain rang through every bone in my body. I could barely think to *move*, let alone to get up.

But I refused to go down that easily. Especially at the hands of Octavia. She had to have been behind the attack, since she had elemental power over water.

I pushed through the pain and forced myself to sit up, surveying the scene around me.

Julian and Vulcan's champion—a guy whose name I forgot but who was gifted with elemental control over fire—fought near one of the horses. Julian wielded two longswords as Vulcan's champion used both hands to throw fireball after fireball at him. Julian expertly used his swords to fend off each ball of fire that came his way.

They both moved so fast that I could barely follow what was happening between them.

Octavia and Antonia battled it out near another horse. Antonia held a bow and arrow, a quiver strapped to her back. She pulled seemingly endless arrows out of the quiver and shot them at Octavia.

But Octavia created a shield of ice to protect herself against the arrows. Then she produced icicles out of thin air with her other hand, shooting them toward Antonia just as Antonia shot arrows toward her.

Antonia easily avoided the icicles.

So Octavia pelted Antonia with a stream of water, knocking Antonia off her feet so her back crashed down on the ground. Before Antonia had a chance to get up, Octavia shot four icicles through her hands and feet, pinning her in place.

Octavia jumped on the horse and rode past Felix, holding out her hand and pulling him up with her. He slipped gracefully behind her, wrapped his arms around her waist, and the two of them galloped off into the sunset.

Now I knew whose side Felix was on.

Mercury's champion—a guy with white wings whose name I also forgot—almost made it to the other horse.

But the ground cracked open in front of him, stopping him in his tracks as thick vines coiled out of the dirt and wrapped themselves around his ankles.

Cassia. She sauntered toward him, green magic and large rocks swirling around her like she was an earth goddess.

Mercury's champion tried to fly free, but the vines held on tightly. And now, as Cassia got closer, she pelted her rocks toward him.

White magic shot out of his palm, knocking the stones out of the way before they could reach him. His magic swirled and gathered around his other hand, and he blew gusts of wind at Cassia to slow her approach. During all of this, he flew up so he was a foot above the ground and pulled on the vines holding him down, stretching them so tight that they looked like they were about to snap.

If they broke, he'd get to the horse before Cassia.

I needed to help her.

Everyone was too caught up in their own battles to pay me any attention. They must have thought Octavia's blast of water had put me down for the count, like it had for Antonia, who was still pinned to the ground by Octavia's icicles. The icicles were starting to melt, but Antonia was unconscious. Probably from the pain.

I glanced at Julian, who was still holding his own against Vulcan's champion. I wasn't sure why I wasted time checking on him, but relief coursed through me when I saw that his sword was close to slicing through one of Vulcan's champion's arms.

Then I heard a snap, and I turned back to where Cassia was fighting Mercury's champion. He'd freed one ankle from the vines. The other didn't look far behind.

He was focused on his fight with Cassia, which meant I had one chance to catch him by surprise. After that, he'd know I was coming for him.

My magic sparked and crackled under my skin. Jolts of it buzzed through my body, ready for action.

But I made sure not to gather *too* much magic. Too much, and I'd kill him instead of knocking him unconscious.

Luckily, chosen champions were as resilient as full-blooded fae. I'd practiced this on Finn. I could do this.

I raced forward, grabbed onto his ankle, and released my electricity into him.

He screamed, his back arching so his chest pointed up to the sky. Bright bolts of lightning lit up his skin. A final rush of wind burst forth from his palms, then his eyes rolled back into his head, and he collapsed onto the ground.

He was splayed out on the grass, motionless. He looked dead.

I rushed toward him and pressed my fingers to his

neck to check for a pulse.

It was weak, but there. Relief crashed through me at the confirmation that I hadn't electrocuted him to death.

I looked up at Cassia. She'd stopped pelting rocks, but green magic still swirled around her, rocks mixed within it.

She eyed me cautiously, like she wasn't sure if she should celebrate the win against Mercury's champion or defend herself against me.

I stood up and shook out my skirt, which was soaked from Octavia's water blast. "You did an amazing job holding him off," I said with a smile. "Want to share the horse?"

Before she could answer, a deep, agonized scream came from where Julian was fighting Vulcan's champion.

Cassia and I twisted our heads to see what had happened.

Julian stood over Vulcan's champion. He held his swords over his head, both of them glistening with blood.

Vulcan's champion sat on the ground and stared at his arms, his eyes wide in horror. Because his arms ended in bloodied stumps below his elbows. His severed hands were on the ground near his feet.

Without his hands, he couldn't use his magic.

He screamed again and lunged for Julian.

Julian held his swords up in an x, stopping him. "Do you want to lose your feet, too?" he asked calmly. Too calmly. As if he did this on a regular basis.

Vulcan's champion growled at him. He didn't back down, but he didn't move forward to attack, either.

"You don't have a shot at getting the wreath without your magic," Julian continued. "But you put up an impressive fight. If I become Emperor of the Villa this week, you have my word that I won't send you to the arena."

Vulcan's champion stared him down. "You swear it?" he asked.

"Yes." Julian lowered his swords. "I swear it."

Vulcan's champion said nothing for a few seconds. "Fine," he gave in. "Take the horse. But I expect you to hold up your end of the bargain." His tone was threatening, his meaning clear.

If Julian didn't keep his word, Vulcan's champion was coming for him.

Julian nodded in respect and swung himself onto the horse.

Suddenly, Vulcan's champion bolted toward the horse near Cassia and me. I wasn't sure how he could ride without his hands, but apparently that wouldn't stop him from trying.

Cassia spun to face him, held a hand out, and shot a rock at his head.

It hit his forehead with a thud.

His head lolled in a circle, and he fell to the ground in a heap.

"Nice one." I gave Cassia an approving nod, and she smiled in return. "So, what do you say?" I asked again, tilting my head toward the horse. "Want to share?"

Her green magic dimmed around her. "I'd love to," she said.

We hopped onto the horse together, sharing it like Octavia had done with Felix. I had my own unicorn on Avalon and was experienced on horseback, so I took the front.

Julian didn't take off on his horse until Cassia and I were situated on ours.

Strange. It was like he was making sure we were set to go before taking off. It was almost like he cared.

Or maybe he was just sizing up his competition.

He was seriously driving me insane. So I shook all thoughts of him away as I grabbed onto the horse's mane, pressed my heels into its sides, and galloped off behind him.

We might have been last out of the gate.

But at least we were still in the running.

42

SELENA

THE SUN HAD FINISHED SETTING by the time we arrived in the capital city. A beautiful aurora danced in the sky, as it had every night since I'd arrived in the Otherworld. But tonight the aurora's lights were particularly bright, with pink and purple mixed in with the usual green.

It was like the sky was celebrating the first competition of the Faerie Games.

Faeries lined the streets, watching as we made our way toward the forum. They clapped as we trotted by— Julian on the horse ahead, and me and Cassia on the horse behind. Everyone in the citadel was under a spell so they wouldn't say anything to help us in the Games, meaning none of them screamed strategic advice at us as we passed.

They parted as we made our way into the forum,

revealing the last person I'd expected to see in the center of it.

Juno sat on the same peacock throne from earlier. She wore the same deep blue dress, although now she held a golden scepter with a swirling blue crystal orb on top of it. It was similar to Bacchus's pinecone scepter, but it looked much more magical.

Her face gave away no emotion as the three of us hopped off our horses and approached her. "Congratulations for making it to this point in the competition," she said. If she was holding a grudge against me for the events of the morning, she didn't show it. "The golden wreath has yet to be claimed. So one of the three of you still has a chance at becoming Emperor of the Villa for the week."

Julian's ice blue eyes glinted with determination. "That's good to know," he said.

"Indeed," Juno said. "You'll have to ride north to the Tomb of the First Queen to find the wreath. Once you're there, getting to the wreath won't be easy."

"I'd expect nothing else," Julian said, already moving to get back onto his horse.

"Each of you will need a sword crafted by Vulcan's own hands," she continued, stopping Julian before he got back onto his horse. He returned to where he'd been standing before her and waited respectfully for her to finish. "Not even the magic gifted to you by Mars can pull such a sword from the godly realm." She looked at Julian, since one of his gifts was the ability to pull any blade he wanted from what looked to be nowhere.

Apparently, "nowhere" was the realm of the gods.

"Where can we find these swords?" I asked.

"That's where I come in," she said. "As you know, gods with a chosen champion in the Games aren't allowed to interact with the players. This keeps them from manipulating the odds to their champion's favor. So I'm here to deliver Vulcan's swords to you."

She pointed the end of her scepter to the ground by her feet and moved it slowly in a circle. As she did, the blue inside the glass orb swirled brighter and faster. It extended out of the orb, creating a sparkling glow of magic where she was drawing the circle. The glow intensified until it was nearly blinding, and then Juno pulled the scepter back to her side.

The magic shimmered and disappeared, revealing three swords at her feet. The blades glowed orange, like they'd just been pulled out of a furnace. Except unlike blades pulled from a furnace, these didn't cool down.

At least there were sheaths beside them—probably so whoever carried the swords didn't burn themselves.

"Good luck," Juno said, and then she turned to me. "I

hope you prove I made the correct decision by letting you continue on in the Games."

"I will," I promised.

She nodded, as if she already knew I would.

The three of us reached for the swords, each of us taking one for ourselves.

After seeing Julian fight Vulcan's champion with two swords, I worried he might take two for himself and leave us in the dust. But he didn't.

Maybe he wasn't so bad after all.

We put on our sheaths and shoved the swords inside of them. Then I turned to Cassia and Julian. "So," I said. "Do either of you know which way is north?"

I knew Avalon like the back of my hand. But the Otherworld? Not so much.

Cassia looked up at the night sky. "The North Star is there." She pointed to a bright star near the Big Dipper. "So the Tomb is that way."

Not wanting to leave without saying goodbye to Juno, I turned back to her and lowered into a curtsy. "Thank you, Your Highness," I said, bowing my head respectfully.

She gave me a tight smile—the first expression she'd shown since we arrived at the forum. "There's no need to call me that," she said, sounding amused. "Such honorifics were created long after the birth of the gods."

"Oh." I bit my lip, mortified at having incorrectly addressed her in two different circumstances. Not just in front of her, but with the entire Otherworld watching on the orbs. "How should I address you, then?"

"By my name." She sat straighter, her scepter gleaming beside her. "Juno."

So the gods went by their first names—like Madonna and Beyoncé. Cool. I could get behind that.

"All right," I said. "Thank you, Juno."

She nodded in acceptance of my thanks, serious once more.

"Come on," Julian urged, focusing on Cassia and me. "The others are likely already close to the Tomb. If we want a shot at the wreath, we need to hurry."

And so, we hopped back onto our horses and rode north toward the Tomb of the First Queen.

SELENA

THE TOMB of the First Queen was fifty miles away from the capital city—twice as far as the distance between the capital city and Vesta's Villa. The journey would have taken eight hours on regular horseback.

But while these horses didn't have wings, they still had magic. They ran at a speed closer to the unicorns on Avalon than the horses on Earth. So we got there in two hours instead of eight.

The horses came to an abrupt stop at the bottom of a tall hill. Like pretty much everywhere in the Otherworld, the hill was covered with thick green grass. I'd thought Avalon was green, but it had nothing on the Otherworld.

"The Tomb's over the top of the hill," Cassia said,

giving our horse's sides a firm but kind kick. "Come on, girl. Not much farther to go."

Both our horse and Julian's horse refused to budge.

Julian jumped off his horse, as graceful as ever. No guy had the right to look that perfect all the time. Especially one I shouldn't be crushing on but was anyway.

"Looks like we're walking the rest of the way," he said, looking to the top of the hill.

"Looks like it," I agreed, and Cassia and I jumped off our horse, too. We patted our horse's nose, thanking her for bringing us that far.

The moment after we did, both our horse and Julian's horse galloped off in the other direction.

"I'd say they were going back to get the champions left behind at the villa," Cassia said, even though the champions left behind were in no condition to continue on in the competition. "But they're heading the wrong way."

"The gods must not want us leaving this place until one of us has the wreath," Julian said.

I nodded, although my stomach fluttered with nerves. It sounded like whatever we were going to face was terrifying enough that the gods worried we might try to flee.

That didn't sound good.

We started up the hill, Julian at one of my sides and

Cassia at the other. None of us said a word as we walked.

"So, who was this First Queen?" I asked, breaking the awkward silence between the three of us.

"Queen Gloriana was the first faerie queen of the Otherworld," Cassia said, happy to jump into telling the story. "Legend says she was the kindest queen to ever rule. But right after she announced that she'd met her soulmate and the two were going to marry, a half-blood killed her. The half-blood was her lover, and he was so overcome with jealousy that he lost his mind. He killed himself right afterward. It's one of the greatest tragedies in the history of the Otherworld."

"After the First Queen was murdered, the faeries started binding the magic of half-bloods and turning us into slaves," Julian added, his eyes hard with anger. "One half-blood committed a crime thousands of years ago, and the rest of us have been paying for it since."

"Wow." My chest hurt at the thought of the half-bloods who'd had to endure such mistreatment for so long. "So the faeries are afraid of the half-bloods. But faeries are so powerful. I imagine it's nearly impossible to kill them."

"It's not impossible," Julian said. "The life source of a faerie exists within their wings. So does ours now, since we're chosen champions. Wings originate from the heart. Destroy the heart, and the faerie—or chosen champion—dies, too."

"Just like a vampire," I said.

"A what?" Cassia asked.

Right. The faeries returned to the Otherworld in the fifth century—which was *before* the original vampires were created on Earth. If any faeries knew about vampires, they either kept it secret from most everyone else in the Otherworld, or just kept it secret from the half-bloods.

"Vampires are one of the supernatural species' that live on Earth," I started. "My father's a vampire."

From there, I told them all about vampires and their abilities.

Cassia couldn't get past the fact that vampires drank blood to survive. She found it vile, even when I told her about the vampires in the Haven that drank animal blood instead of human blood.

I was still telling them about vampires when we approached the crest of the hill. But then I saw it, and I stopped speaking—and walking—mid-sentence.

Because straight ahead of us were the backs of three giant, furry heads. They were so close together that they clearly shared a body. And even though it was only the back of it, I'd learned enough in Ancient Magical History 101 to guess what this monster was.

Cerberus. The vicious, three-headed dog that guarded the gates to the Beyond. Well, here they called it the Underworld. But it seemed like they were just two different words that described the same thing—the place where people went after death.

Julian pulled his glowing sword out of its sheath, holding it at the ready. Cassia and I did the same.

"Cerberus is guarding the entrance of the Tomb," Julian said, softly as to not catch the three-headed monster's attention. "We'll have to kill him to get to the wreath."

"We can do that?" I asked. "Just kill an infamous monster that's been around for..." I tried to figure out how long Cerberus must have been around, but couldn't come up with anything. "Since the beginning of time?"

"Cerberus belongs in the Underworld," Julian said. "Pluto must have sent him here for this competition. So by killing him here, we're sending him back to his home, where he belongs."

"Great," I said, still not confident we could do this. Yes, we were powerful after being gifted with magic from the gods. But Cerberus was a monster as old as time itself.

"Don't look so worried." Julian gave me a reassuring smile, as if he knew what was going through my mind. "Emperor of the Villa competitions aren't designed to kill us. The gods want the fights to the death to happen in the arena. So Cerberus will know to leave us alive. He can injure us—badly—but nothing he'll do to us will be fatal."

"That's good to know," I muttered. Although I supposed from the perspective of the gods and the faeries, it made sense. It would be far more *entertaining* for them to watch each Emperor of the Villa choose which three chosen champions to send to the arena.

This whole thing was sick. But I couldn't let my mind go there. Because right now, I had to stop the champions who'd left the villa before us—mainly Octavia—from getting that wreath.

The three of us crept around the Tomb, which was basically a smaller hill on top of the larger hill. As we approached Cerberus's side, I realized he looked more terrifying than I'd imagined.

I'd always pictured him as a giant, three-headed dog. But he was more like a giant, three-headed *wolf*. All six of his eyes glowed yellow, his incisors were almost as long as my arms, and his claws were sharpened into points.

His heads focused away from us, and he growled and bared his teeth, ready to attack.

Maybe he'd heard our horses going that way? But that distraction wouldn't protect us for long.

Luckily, there were chains around his necks, keeping him tied to the Tomb. Unfortunately, he was standing right in front of the entrance, so we still had to get past him to get inside.

We made our way around the Tomb, and I saw the chosen champions who'd arrived before us. Molly, Cillian, Octavia, and Felix.

They were covered in strange black goo, and were splayed out on the field in front of Cerberus. Judging from the way they weren't moving, they were all unconscious.

The only champion missing was Bridget. Had she already gotten the wreath?

She couldn't have. If she had, Bacchus would have announced her as the winner, and the champions splayed out in front of us would be healed.

She must have run away. Or she was purposefully staying under the radar, like I was supposed to be doing.

"What happened to them?" I asked, my gaze roaming over the bodies of the fallen champions again.

"It looks like some kind of poison," Julian said. "Cerberus must have spat it at them, and it knocked them out."

"Great." My stomach lurched at the knowledge that all of the players before us had fought Cerberus and failed.

Cerberus must have heard us talking, because all three of his heads turned in our direction at once. I could have almost sworn that they all smiled at the sight of us. Then the middle one bared its teeth and growled. The other two joined in, and together, they pawed their front legs into the ground, sharp claws slicing through the dirt.

If not for the chains, I had a feeling he would have pounced by now. As it was, I backed up, not wanting to risk being anywhere the monster could reach. Julian and Cassia followed suit.

How were we supposed to beat Cerberus? I had no idea. But I forced myself to breathe steadily, trying to calm my racing heart. Panicking wasn't going to help anything.

Plus, being knocked unconscious wasn't the worst thing in the world. It beat dying.

We'd already gotten this far in the competition. We had nothing to lose by trying to beat Cerberus and getting into that Tomb.

Once we got inside, I had to make sure Cassia got the wreath instead of Julian. She was the only one I trusted to keep me out of the arena this week.

"So," I said, trying to sound more relaxed than I felt. "How do we kill this thing?"

"Cutting off the heads usually does the trick." Julian

held up his fiery sword and admired it, as if he was already picturing slicing the blade through Cerberus's thick necks. "These swords must be the only ones that can cut through its skin."

"They must," Cassia agreed.

Although from looking at the matching swords strewn next to the fallen champions' bodies, it didn't look like that technique had worked for them.

"A three-pronged attack will work best," Julian continued, apparently not sharing my worry. Of course he didn't. His patron god was Mars—the god of war. Fighting was his specialty. "I'll take the middle head. Selena will take the right, and Cassia will take the left. And remember—if Cerberus looks like he's about to spit out poison, avoid it at all costs. It's better to be delayed than unconscious."

"Right." I nodded, reminding myself that even though Cerberus was massive, the extra strength I'd gotten with my new magic allowed me to jump high enough to reach him. "We go on three?"

"On three." Julian held my gaze and nodded. His fiery blade reflected in his eyes, making him look as fierce and dangerous as ever. "One, two—"

"Wait!" Cassia held out her arms, stopping us before Julian could say three.

"What?" I looked at her, worried she was about to chicken out.

But her green eyes were wide with excitement, like she'd just had an idea.

"Fighting Cerberus was one of Hercules's twelve labors," she said quickly. "But Hercules didn't kill Cerberus. He did something else..." She paused and stared up at the aurora dancing in the sky, trying and apparently failing to remember the rest of the story.

As she was thinking, someone with sparkly gold wings zoomed out of the shadows and stopped in front of us. Bridget. She was covered in mud, but other than that, she appeared uninjured.

"You're right," Bridget said, looking approvingly at Cassia. "Hercules didn't kill Cerberus. And if you try to kill him, you're going to end up just like the rest of the fallen champions on that field."

44

SELENA

"IF YOU KNOW how to beat Cerberus, why haven't you done it yourself?" I asked, instantly suspicious of Bridget's motives.

The golden orbs circled around us, eating up every word of our conversation.

"Because while Hercules was able to fight Cerberus alone, that's because he's an extraordinarily strong demigod," she said. "We're strong, but nothing in comparison to Hercules. And while Julian's right about a three-pronged attack being the best way to go about this task, he's wrong about the task being to kill Cerberus. Because to get past Cerberus, we need to use the same method as Hercules."

"I'm guessing they used the wrong method?" I glanced at the fallen champions on the field.

"Correct," Bridget said. "Molly tried to touch Cerberus so she could learn the feel of his form and shift into it. He swatted her away with his claws, and she used her sword to protect herself. The moment she drew blood, it burst out of the wound, splashing her and knocking her out."

"So that's what the black goo is," Cassia said. "Blood."

"Yep," Bridget said. "Cerberus's blood is poisonous enough to knock us out, but not quite strong enough to kill us. Cillian was the only one who knew the right way to beat Cerberus, but he didn't know about the blood being poison. He's so cocky that he thought he could beat Cerberus on his own. Which he couldn't, since none of us can. The whole point of this part of the competition is to force us to work together. So Cillian tried, failed, and ended up using his sword to protect himself, too."

"Which splattered blood on him and knocked him out," I finished.

Bridget nodded, and continued, "Octavia and Felix arrived next. They attacked the same way you were planning on doing it—by cutting off the heads. The moment their swords drew blood, they were knocked out, too."

Julian studied Bridget the whole time she explained

this to us, his eyes narrowing as she spoke. "Where were you during all this?" he asked.

"The moment I arrived, I covered myself in mud dark enough that in the night, it passes as Cerberus's blood." She motioned to her mud-covered body. "I lay on the ground like the others are now. They thought I'd been knocked out, too. But I was just biding my time until the three of you arrived."

"Why us?" I asked. "If three champions have to work together to beat Cerberus, why didn't you work with Octavia and Felix when they arrived?"

"Octavia is ruthless," Bridget said. "I don't trust her, and I never will. Plus, I don't want to fight Cerberus, and I don't want the wreath. At least, not this week."

"If you don't want the wreath, what *do* you want?" I asked. Because in the Faerie Games, everyone always wanted something.

She appraised me with her calm gray eyes. "I want to make a deal," she said. "I'll tell you how to beat Cerberus. But only if you promise that whichever one of you gets the wreath won't send me to the arena this week."

She was offering us an alliance. One that only lasted for a week, but it was something we could build on as the Games continued.

"How do we know that after we beat Cerberus, you

won't bolt into the Tomb and take the wreath for your-self?" I asked.

"Because I meant what I said earlier. I don't want the wreath this week," she said. "I know that if we come to an agreement, all three of you will stick to your word. And that's enough for me. So, what do you say? Do you accept the deal?"

"It's not a bad offer," Julian mused. "But you're asking us to do a lot of dirty work for you. So how about this. We do what you asked of us this week. In return, if you get the wreath in the three weeks following this week, you won't send any of us to the arena."

A four-week alliance. Julian was doing a good job protecting not just himself, but Cassia and me, too. It was surprisingly thoughtful of him.

Or maybe he was just looking out for himself, and the two of us had lucked out by being in the right place at the right time.

That was probably it. But still, I'd take what I could get if it meant a better chance at avoiding the arena for the next few weeks.

Bridget tilted her head, considering his offer. "Two weeks and you have a deal," she said.

"Agreed," Julian said, and then he looked at Cassia and me to see if we were in as well.

"Agreed," we said at the same time.

"Great." Bridget smiled, and our alliance was solidified. "Now, here's what Hercules did to beat Cerberus…"

She told us the story, and from there, we formulated our plan of attack.

45

SELENA

"REMEMBER, Cerberus's poison will wear off eventually, and the other champions will have another shot at fighting him," Bridget reminded us as we got into position. "Cillian knows how to beat Cerberus. He'll likely team up with Octavia and Felix and make a run for the wreath himself, although Octavia will want it, too. So you have one shot to do this right."

If Octavia ended up with the wreath, she'd send me to the arena. I had no doubt about it.

"And watch out for Cerberus's teeth," Bridget said. "They won't knock you out like his blood, but they're poisonous, too. Just a scratch will weaken your magic significantly."

"No problem," Julian said, as confident as ever. "We've got this."

There was a magical shield all around the Tomb, making it impossible to attack Cerberus from behind. So the front it was.

Julian had volunteered to take the center head, so he stood in the middle. I was at his right, and Cassia was at his left. Bridget stood behind us, looking mighty proud of herself for the deal she'd made with us.

Even though she was working with us for the next few weeks, I'd have to be careful around her after that.

We placed our swords and sheaths on the ground, because we wouldn't need them. They were actually a detriment, since they increased our chances of drawing blood and getting knocked unconscious by the poison.

For this challenge, we couldn't use any weapons apart from our own strength and magic. The swords had just been a trick to make the competition more interesting to watch. Which was twisted, but also clever.

It felt strange to be weaponless, but I had my lightning, Cassia had her earth magic, and Julian had his strength. Together, we could do this.

We faced the three growling heads, sizing them up as we got ready to ambush.

Green magic floated out of Cassia's palms and swirled around her, picking up rocks from the ground so the magic and rocks intertwined together. I dug inside myself to ignite my lightning, feeling it spark and crackle under my skin. Julian didn't have to do anything —he was just pure brute force that was dangerous to mess with.

"On three," Julian said, and this time, he counted to three with no interruptions.

Time to attack.

Cassia hurled rocks straight at Cerberus's faces. She put enough force behind the rocks to irritate the monster, but not so much that they drew blood. And to be extra safe, she padded the rocks with her magic to cushion them so they weren't sharp and pointy.

The three heads howled, but the howls turned into whimpers as more and more rocks hit its three ugly faces.

No one liked having rocks thrown at their face—not even giant, legendary monsters from the Underworld.

Once Cerberus was thoroughly irritated, Julian ran toward him, pushed off the ground, and took a flying leap. I did the same, and Cassia followed, no longer throwing rocks as we soared through the air.

I focused on the top of Cerberus's head, which was where I was trying to land. But while I was in mid-air, he raised his paw and swiped it straight at me, swatting me out of the air.

Pain ricocheted through my bones. But I landed on the ground on my back, and my wings padded my fall, making the impact not nearly as bad as it would have been otherwise.

The paw swipe had knocked the wind out of me, but it was nothing I couldn't recover from. So I stood up and brushed the dirt off my dress. But before trying to leap again, I checked on Julian and Cassia.

Julian had landed on top of the center head as planned. He looked like a god, gripping onto the head with his legs and hands as Cerberus bucked his neck, trying unsuccessfully to throw him off.

Cassia hadn't been so lucky. She dangled on the outside part of the neck of the head she'd been aiming for. She clutched onto its fur for dear life... and there was a bloody scratch along her leg that had ripped the bottom side of her skirt in two.

Her green wings dimmed, losing their sparkle until they were a transparent shadow of what they'd been.

Cerberus's teeth had scratched her. Her magic was weakening. If she let go to fall, the impact would surely break her bones. Even if it didn't, she no longer had the magic needed to leap high enough to get near the head again.

To make things worse, the head she was holding onto was trying to buck her off. Her legs flopped through the air like a rag doll, and her grip around the fur was slowly slipping.

"Brace yourself with your feet and climb up!" I called out to her. "You can do it!"

She got her feet situated on the neck to keep herself steadier than before. Once somewhat stable, she reached one hand up to pull herself up like she was scaling a cliff. But her arms shook from the strain, nearly giving up on her. She grunted and tried again. But this attempt was just as unsuccessful as the first.

Before I realized what was happening, Julian leaped from the head he was balancing on to land on the one Cassia was hanging onto. He braced his legs around the head like he'd done before and stretched his arm down to help her.

He was close, but there were still inches between them. And her hands were slipping, and slipping. It wouldn't be long until she lost her grip and crashed to the ground.

Julian scooted as far to the side of the head as possible and stretched farther toward Cassia. His other arm extended outward in the other direction to keep himself from losing his balance. He was holding onto the head using only the strength in his legs, and he was doing it like a pro.

But the center head saw its opportunity, opening its

mouth and salivating as it prepared to chomp Julian's arm straight off.

"No!" I screamed, and seconds before the head bit down on Julian's arm, thick bolts of lightning burst out of my palms and came together to strike Cerberus straight in its center face.

46

SELENA

THE CENTER HEAD FROZE, vibrating like crazy as my lightning electrocuted it.

I held onto the magic with everything I had, not letting go of Cerberus's head. The lightning arced between my hands and the head, crackling and sparking and lighting up everything around us in its brilliant glow.

I gritted my teeth and maintained my hold on the bolts as Julian got a firm grip on Cassia, pulling her up onto the top of the head with him. Relief coursed through me the moment she was up there.

Time for me to try jumping onto my assigned head again.

But right then, one of the fallen champions on the ground started to stir. Molly.

I broke my lightning hold on the center head, kept as much power inside me as I could, and ran toward where Molly was slowly pushing herself up from the ground.

I placed my hand on her shoulder and jolted her with the perfect amount of electricity to knock her out again without killing her.

She slumped back down, unconscious. But it wouldn't be long before the others started waking, too. And I wasn't sure how much voltage to shoot them with while they were still unconscious to make sure not to kill them. For all I knew, the poison had put them on the brink of death and anything more would push them over. I couldn't risk it.

Which meant we needed to take care of Cerberus, quickly.

I backed up, ran toward Cerberus, and leaped onto his right head. He must have been weakened from my lightning, because this time he didn't lash out at me with his paw. He wasn't being as forceful with trying to buck me off like with Cassia and Julian before, either.

I would have shot him with lightning from the beginning if I could create bolts on command. But no—it took Cerberus nearly biting Julian's arm off for me to do more than electrocute with a touch. Just like it had taken an entire crowd booing at me to shoot bolts at those orbs.

Extreme emotions apparently heightened my magic.

Hopefully it was something I'd learn to control sooner rather than later. And hopefully Julian, Cassia, and Bridget wouldn't tell the other champions what I'd just done. I couldn't risk being seen as more of a threat.

After positioning myself on the head so I faced backward, I checked on Julian and Cassia. Julian was on the left head, and Cassia had somehow made it to the center one.

With the center head weakened the most from my lightning, she wouldn't need her full strength to do what came next.

"Is everyone in position?" Julian asked, looking over at Cassia and me. Bridget was still on the ground, pretending to be unconscious.

I tightened my legs around the head and leaned down to wrap my arms around the neck. "Yep!" I said, and Cassia echoed the same.

"Go!" he said, and at his command, I squeezed my arms around Cerberus's neck.

The monster fought me, bucking harder as I cut off his air source. But I didn't let go. I held tighter and tighter, feeling the muscles in his neck strain as he struggled and failed to breathe.

It felt like I was holding on for at least a minute before the head drooped to the ground, unconscious.

Julian's head was unconscious, too. But Cassia was still working on hers, her eyes closed as she mustered as much strength to squeeze harder.

The heads had to be knocked out around the same time for this to work. If the center head continued getting air, the other two would wake quickly.

"You can do it!" I yelled up at Cassia in encouragement. "You're almost there!"

She grunted and tightened her hold around the neck. Within seconds, her head fell unconscious, too.

Just like Hercules, we'd beaten Cerberus using only brute force. The monster was out cold—for now.

As per our plan, we hurried around Cerberus's unconscious body and into the Tomb as quickly as possible. Now that Cerberus was no longer blocking the entrance, I saw it was a cave leading into the hill.

The orbs followed us inside, buzzing around us and providing us with light. For once, I was grateful for their presence.

Cassia lagged behind because of the scratch on her leg. I went to her and held her up by her shoulders, helping her move faster.

Bridget didn't follow behind us. Good. She was being honest about not wanting the wreath. Which meant she could be trusted—at least until our deal expired.

We turned around a corner, and there it was: a statue of a beautiful faerie woman. She must have been Queen Gloriana.

Golden leaves circled around her head.

The Emperor of the Villa wreath.

47

SELENA

I BALANCED on the balls of my feet, ready to hold off Julian if he ran to grab the wreath first.

But none of us moved to take it.

"You should take it," I told Cassia. "You shared the horse with me when you didn't have to, and you went through the most with fighting Cerberus. Plus, if it hadn't been for you stopping us, we would have attacked Cerberus with our swords before Bridget got to us. We'd be covered in black poison, unconscious like the other champions out there. You deserve it."

"I don't want it." She gazed at the wreath, fear gleaming in her eyes. "I trust both of you to keep me safe this week."

I should have known she'd say that. Only the most

impulsive, overconfident champions wanted to be Emperor of the Villa the first week.

Cassia was none of those things.

She was doing exactly what I was supposed to be doing —staying under the radar. That was a game she could play well, unlike me, who'd been on everyone's radars from the start because I was Jupiter's first ever chosen champion.

Julian turned to me, his face hard with resolve. "It'll be better for you if you don't take it," he said. "I'll be Emperor of the Week and keep the two of you—plus Bridget and Vulcan's champion—safe."

Suspicion built in my chest. "Why would you do what's best for me instead of what's best for you?"

"Consider it an apology," he said. "For bringing you to the Otherworld in the first place."

Every muscle in my body stiffened at the unwelcome reminder.

Why should I believe he'd be true to his word if he were Emperor of the Week? He was a liar. Plus, I'd seen him in front of Juno earlier. He wanted that wreath. Badly.

He was using my feelings for him to manipulate me. Again.

I wouldn't be fooled a second time.

"I don't accept your apology," I said, and from the

way his face crumpled, it looked like my words were a punch to his gut.

After what he'd done to me, it shouldn't have hurt me to do that to him. But it did.

"But I stick to my word," I continued. "And I promise not to send you, Cassia, or Bridget to the arena this week. Because I wouldn't be here right now if not for the three of you."

Before I had time to talk myself out of it, I bolted to the statue, plucked the wreath off Queen Gloriana's head, and lowered it on top of mine.

"Congratulations Selena, the chosen champion of Jupiter!" Bacchus's voice announced through the orbs the moment the wreath was secured. "You've won the golden wreath, and are the first Empress of the Villa in this year's Faerie Games!"

As he spoke, the wound on Cassia's leg stitched together and healed. Color came back to her cheeks, and her green wings returned to their full sparkling brightness.

The aches and bruises I'd acquired through the competition immediately felt better, too.

"All chosen champions, please remain where you are," Bacchus instructed. "Your transportation back to Vesta's Villa will arrive shortly. And I know that I— along with the other gods and the citizens of the Otherworld—look forward to seeing Selena decide which three of the ten other champions she'll send to the arena this week!"

He said something more, but I didn't hear him.

Because the wreath felt a million times heavier at the reminder of the awful decision I'd be forced to make within the next few days.

One of the three champions I'd send to the arena would die. I might not be the one to physically kill them, but his or her blood would be on my hands.

And the two that survived?

They'd be coming for me.

48

JACEN

"I'M GOING to save our daughter," I promised, holding onto Annika's hands as I gazed into her beautiful golden eyes. "No matter what it takes."

We stood together in our quarters in the castle. My wife was one of the strongest women I knew, but with our daughter's life at stake, she looked more vulnerable than ever.

Her magic was bound to Avalon, so she couldn't leave. If she did, the magic that protected our island would fail, and the demons lurking on Earth would surely locate us and attack.

Bella was in our quarters, too, waiting by the crackling fireplace. She was going to teleport me to the crossroads whenever I was ready. Because despite all the research we'd done and all the allies we'd reached out to, going to the crossroads with the fresh blood of someone you'd killed was the only answer we'd found for how to reach the fae.

I already had the necessary blood in a vial with me. Earlier, Bella had teleported me to the Devereux mansion in LA, where the Devereux witches imprisoned murderers they'd captured in their basement. Blood was necessary for the strongest dark magic spells, and that was their somewhat ethical way of acquiring it.

Once there, I'd done what I had to do, put the blood I'd need in the vial, and left the rest for the witches to use however they saw fit.

"I trust you, and I look forward to seeing our daughter soon," Annika said. "But we have to be prepared that we might not be able to contact the fae until the next full moon."

Right. The annoying catch that came up in every mention of going to the crossroads to call upon the fae. You were *only* supposed to go on the night of the full moon.

But that was over a week away.

No books and no person alive knew what happened if you went on any other night.

"I have to try," I said. "Who knows what's happening to Selena in the Otherworld? We can't wait for the full moon."

"I know," Annika said. "I love you. And be safe."

"I love you, too." I placed a light kiss on her lips, not caring that Bella was watching. "I'll see you soon."

She nodded, although her beautiful eyes shined with worry.

I was just as worried for our daughter. But despite not having any magic, Selena was smart and creative. She'd figure out how to stay alive until help came for her.

And that was what I intended on asking the fae that met me at the crossroads—how to travel from Earth to the Otherworld.

By kidnapping my daughter, the Otherworld had all but declared war on Avalon. Once I learned how to get to the faerie realm, the army on Avalon would march into the Otherworld, and we wouldn't leave until Selena was back home where she belonged.

I had no more time to waste. So while it physically pained me to pull away from Annika, I did it, walking over to where Bella was waiting.

"You ready?" Bella held out her hands for me to take.

"Yes." I placed my hands firmly in hers, feeling more determined than ever. "Let's go save my daughter."

She nodded, and then the world flashed out around us as we disappeared into the ether.

The crossroads were in Ireland's Ancient East, at a place called Loughcrew Cairns. Despite being a bit over an hour away from the major city of Dublin, Loughcrew Cairns was full of green land for as far as the eye could see. It was sparsely populated, minus the busloads of tourists that came through to see the faerie trees and tombs.

Neither tourists nor locals came to the crossroads. Not because the crossroads weren't beautiful. With a clear sparkling lake in the center, chirping birds, colorful flowers, and a large faerie tree with branches like umbrellas full of leaves, the crossroads were absolutely stunning.

But the crossroads emitted powerful magic—magic that repelled people. Only those in the know, those daring enough to risk a deal with the fae, came here.

Bella and I teleported smack into the middle of a circle of glowing rocks that made up a faerie ring. Outside the faerie ring, misty rain fell softly on the grass. Inside the faerie ring, the weather was perfect. Although the sky was cloudy, so I couldn't see the moon.

But I knew it wasn't full.

Bella handed me the small bowl I'd need to use to create the mixture to call upon the fae. "I'm going to step off to the side," she said. "But I'll be ready to help in case anything goes wrong."

"Nothing will go wrong," I said.

"I hope not. However, you have backup if it does."

I nodded, watching her move away to stand near the faerie tree. Once she was in place, I walked up to the bushes near the shimmering lake, picked exactly thirty-three red berries from their leaves, and put them in the bowl. Next, I dumped the vial of the blood from the human I'd killed in with the berries. Lastly, I picked a nearby rose and pricked my finger with one of its thorns.

"I want to learn a permanent, unchanging way that all creatures of Earth can use to get from Earth to a currently safe place that's populated with faeries in the Otherworld," I said as I dropped thirty-three drops of my blood into the bowl.

The question was pointed and specific, since faeries were known for twisting their deals. If I only asked for a way to get to the Otherworld, they'd likely tell me a way that used to exist but has been closed off for centuries, or lead me to an unsafe place where I'd be ambushed by a hoard of monsters. I didn't want to give them an opportunity to avoid giving me the answer I needed.

With the stem of the rose, I stirred the mixture until the berries were soaked in the blood. Then I removed each berry one by one and tossed them into the shimmering lake, watching as they drifted to the bottom.

All was quiet. I stared into the water, my skin prickling in the breeze as I waited for *something* to happen.

"Prince Jacen Pearce," a light, airy female voice said from behind me. "I've been expecting you."

Want to discover along with Jacen why it's a terrible idea to call on the fae when the moon isn't full?

Sign up for my mailing list, and an extra scene that takes place immediately following the end of this book will be sent straight to your inbox!

To grab the extra scene, CLICK HERE or visit http:// michellemadow.com/faerie-games-extra-scene.

You'll be subscribing to my email list to get the extra scene. I love connecting with my readers and promise not to spam you, but you're free to unsubscribe at any time.

The Faerie Games is the first book in what's going to be an EPIC series. The second book—*The Faerie Pawn*—is OUT NOW!

Grab *The Faerie Pawn* on Amazon → CLICK HERE

ABOUT *THE FAERIE PAWN* (You may have to turn the page to see the cover and description)

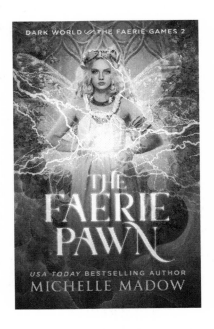

I need to learn how to control my new magic—before

it gets me killed.

As the first ever Faerie Games player gifted with magic from the king of the gods—Jupiter—all eyes are on me. Especially since I won the first competition of the Games. Now I need to send three other players to fight in the Coliseum until one of them is dead.

The two that survive will be gunning for me later. So I need to choose my alliances carefully. And as much as I hate to admit it, the magnetically attractive Julian is tempting me to work with him moving forward.

I *should* hate Julian, since he kidnapped me to the Otherworld in the first place. But he's helping me learn how to control my new magic. And I'm drawn to him on a level I don't understand.

One player will win the Faerie Games and survive. The rest will die.

I need to win. If that means getting close to Julian… then that's exactly what I'm going to do.

Grab *The Faerie Pawn* on Amazon → CLICK HERE

I love connecting with and chatting with my readers online! Here are the places where you can find me:

Facebook Group ➜ https://www.facebook.com/groups/michellemadow

Instagram ➜ https://www.instagram.com/michellemadow (@michellemadow)

Hope to see you around! :)

ABOUT THE AUTHOR

Michelle Madow is a USA Today bestselling author of fast-paced fantasy novels that will leave you turning the pages wanting more! Her books are full of magic, adventure, romance, and twists you'll never see coming.

Click here or visit author.to/MichelleMadow to view a full list of Michelle's novels on Amazon.

To get free books, exclusive content, and instant updates from Michelle, visit http://bit.ly/madowsubscribe and subscribe to her newsletter now!

THE FAERIE GAMES

Published by Dreamscape Publishing

Copyright © 2019 Michelle Madow

ISBN: 9781088510322

✤ Created with Vellum